METAL MONSTERS

Metal Monsters

G.D. Stark

Published by Castalia House
Tampere, Finland
www.castaliahouse.com

Cover: Steve Beaulieu
Editor: Vox Day
Created by Vox Day

ISBN: 978-952-7065-10-5

Contents

Prologue

Ioannes Laedon lay in bed, watching the sky lighten to purple as a pink sliver of sun rose above the mountains. He'd chosen this apartment for the view alone. From its location high above the city, its floor-to-ceiling window commanded a stunning view of the bay and the craggy snow-capped peaks of the great Makken range that surrounded it. It felt luxurious, though the building itself was a typically severe block of utilitarian engineering, complete with exposed pipes, communal showers and very little in the way of privacy or personal space. Ioannes stroked his wife's hair with his left hand.

"Why are you awake, Io?" Kaly mumbled at him. "You're worse than those damn birds!"

He patted her on the head and said nothing. He was technically on call right now, but outside of the occasional drill, there hadn't ever been an actual surface-to-space scramble that he could recall. His apartment was located only three blocks from the spaceport, so instead of staying on base like some of his colleagues, he stayed with his family and enjoyed the perks of civilization. Not to mention a little one-on-one time with Kaly.

Laedon rolled out of bed and stretched, then went to the kitchen and grabbed one of his precious stash of *ZZZgone!* energy drinks out of the refrigerator. Imports were expensive and he rationed his luxuries but today felt like a holiday. He just had some reports to finish, then he planned to take his two boys, Ioannes Jr. and little Erasmus, to the bay for an afternoon of fishing. His on-call schedule ended at noon, then the rest of the day would be wide open.

He grabbed a yeast bar from the cabinet and ate it as he pulled up the local news on the dining room table's projector. Factory shut down by runaway welding bot, grain futures trending down due to excellent harvests, a statement from the Lords on new labor regulations, nothing of any interest to him. He washed down the last bite of the bar with a swallow of *ZZZgone!* and switched to the interstellar news so he could check the slingball stats. Nice, he thought. The Reavers edged out the 'Saurs. That'd be good for the Salamanders' standing in the EC. Hope they sign Fokker before he gets picked up by someone else. If they can pull that off, they'll be set for–

His thought was interrupted as his transceiver pinged an alert. No way—they're seriously calling me in today?

"This is Sergeant Laedon," he said after quickly calling in.

"We've got multiple unidentified craft entering the system," the dispatcher said. His familiar voice sounded unusually stressed.

"This a drill?"

"We've gone to max alert. What do you think? Better get in here now!"

"Roger that," Laedon said. He took a deep breath to calm his suddenly racing heart, then went to grab his uniform and sidearm from his bedroom.

"What is it?" Kaly asked from the bed, squinting at him.

"Dispatch called," he replied, walking over and kissing her on the forehead. "Tell the boys I'll take them fishing another time. It's probably just a drill, but it could take all day. I'll let you know as soon as it's over."

"Be safe, baby," she told him, pushing her hair out of her eyes. But he'd already left.

Laedon checked in to the base eight minutes later and found his decade. Most of them were little more than half-awake, and several were, at best, hung over.

"We may have a false alarm here," Overseer Thallos informed them, "but SSD is reporting a squadron of deep space vessels incoming."

"Space systems defense is reporting incoming enemy?" said a nervous voice. "An invasion?" It was Trykos, the base's pet journalist from the *Laconian Free Press*.

"Yes," Thallos said. "It's almost certainly the end of the world. Now shut up when I'm addressing the men or I'll bounce you out of here no matter what clearances you've got." He turned to the unit. "All we know at this point is that the *Nikolaos* is sitting between us and what appear to be two troop transports and a handful of fighter escorts."

The *Nikolaos* was a modern cruiser, unveiled with much fanfare the previous year. She was more than suited for planetary defense; unfortunately, she was the only deep space defense the Stratocracy had. Even so, a handful of fighters and some troop transports wouldn't be a problem for her, should they prove hostile. But who were they anyhow, and how was it possible that SSD hadn't ID'd them yet?

"If the transports make it through we'll nail them on the surface," Paulson continued. "This doesn't make much sense from what I'm seeing. It's probably just pirate activity again, or maybe a group of asylum seekers fleeing a war somewhere. I'll keep you apprised. Ready transports and weapons for intercept on the surface."

After relaying the telemetry on the incoming ships to SSD Command, Captain Marinos ordered his crew to battle stations. On the long range scans, the two incoming transports and their eight light-fighter escorts did not appear to be intimidating. But the incoming ships hadn't responded to the automated warning beacon or given any ID when hailed. They simply approached in silence, apparently without concern for any systems defenses, which made Marinos wonder what game they were playing. It would be a good test of the *Nikolaos*, though. Shooting down asteroids and clearing the planetary orbit of space junk lost its charm after a few weeks in space.

"Three minutes to torpedo range," Ensign Cloris announced from his recon station.

"All shields at maximum, ready one salvo of torpedoes," Marinos said. "Strap in, gentlemen."

The bridge around him was modern and comfortable, with smooth edges and indirect lighting. Somehow it never felt right to Marinos, who had cut his teeth on an old Class II destroyer inherited from the Valatestan Navy, with its exposed oxygen tubes, outmoded digitals, and disturbingly green interior lighting. The *Nikolaos* felt like an interior design catalog in comparison. Its weapons were state-of-the-art TL-14 with a full bank of plasma cannons, torpedoes and shielding capable of keeping the ship cool while passing through the corona of a sun. It even had seatbelts.

Marinos keyed the com. "Attention approaching vessels. This is Captain Lukas Marinos of the *Nikolaos*. Shut down your engines or you will be fired upon. This is your last warning. Repeat—stand down now or you will be destroyed."

"No response," Cloris announced. "Wait—we've got two fighters picking up speed, outpacing the transports, moving into attack formation—damn, they're fast! They're coming for us, sir."

"Hold your course, Helmsman Lunis," Marinos said to the man to his right.

PO Eustis spoke from his weapons console. "Coming into plasma range in four… three… two… one… in range!"

"How many have a shot?"

"All the odd, less number one."

"Fire all five!" Marinos said. "Take 'em out!"

The first fighter came in fast but the *Nikolaos* tore her to shreds with her plasma cannons before she could get in a shot. The second fighter banked hard to avoid the hail of searing energy and barely made it back out of range of the *Nikolaos's* cannons as the five cannons spat heated fury in her direction.

"They choked on that!" Cloris laughed.

"Ready two torpedo salvos—nail those transports. First the one to spinward, then the other. We can pick off the fighters later."

A button was pressed and four deadly missiles flew from the mouth of *Nikolaos*. Tipped with armor shattering warheads, they were AI-controlled and capable of hitting 1/10 light speed only four seconds after launch. There was a pause, and then the ship belched forth another four. Marinos watched the tactical display as the torpedoes locked on their targets—four per transport for the sake of redundancy. By the book.

POP—the torpedoes engaged their pulse drives—and then… nothing. The red dots of the transports did not vanish as expected, but continued on their path towards the planet as if nothing had happened.

"Where are the torps?" Marinos gasped in amazement. "Where are they?"

"I don't know," Eustis said. "They disappeared!"

"What?" Marinos said. "All eight? You can't see them?"

"They're gone, sir. Shall we fire two more salvos?"

Marinos felt ice in his guts. It was impossible—the very speed of those torpedoes and the AI locks—there was no way! Something was wrong. But what?

"Not yet. No point in wasting eight more when we don't know what's going on."

"Sir!" Cloris said. "Fighters coming back! Two!"

"Ready cannons, Eustis—fire as soon as they're in range. Smoke them!"

The fighters flew in close to the edge of *Nikolaos's* firing range but they'd learned from the first encounter. They split and tore around the perimeter of the ship. The plasma cannons opened up on them, but the range was far enough that the fighters' shields held.

"What are they doing?" Marinos asked as he watched the small red dots zip around the perimeter on opposite sides of *Nikolaos*.

"They're firing!" Cloris announced. "Looks like some sort of small projectiles or micro missiles."

They were coming in too fast for the anti-missile lasers, but they were so small that even nuclear-tipped warheads would barely scratch the ship's armor.

"We got a few," Cloris said, swiping through screens on his console. "Most were small enough to slip past. Eight impacts. No real damage, though. All systems still 100 percent."

"Excellent," Marinos said, watching as the two fighters rounded the ship and returned to their previous formation around the transports. "Let's get closer and take out those transports with our cannon—they gotta be jamming our missiles somehow. We know the plasma works."

"Roger, Captain," Helmsman Lunis said, setting a course. He pressed his fingers on his console multiple times in growing frustration. "Sir—my console—it's jammed up."

"Cloris?" Marinos said. Cloris opened his secondary screen and tried to set the course himself. After a few seconds he shook his head. "Sir, I've also lost the ability to–"

The lights blinked out on the bridge and strips of red light appeared on the floor, lighting the way to the exits.

"What the devil?" Cloris said.

The main viewscreen went to a solid blue screen reading SYSTEM RESTART. CONTINUE?

"No!" Marinos said. "Don't restart!"

As he said it, half the screen dissolved into static.

Lunis cursed loudly, jerking backwards at his console. "I just got shocked!"

"Sir!" Cloris announced. "Life support is shutting down—the automatic bulkheads are going to seal!"

VENTING ATMOSPHERE, announced the ship. *ALL AIRLOCKS OPENING IN TWO MINUTES.*

"Sir," Cloris said. "We have no control over the engines or the helm—we're now on a course directly for Owannis."

Owannis was the planet's third moon.

"What?" Marinos shouted. "Seal those airlocks!" He stabbed at the console in front of him, trying to see the ship's course. The screen blinked white, then black—dead!

"We're accelerating, sir," Cloris said calmly.

90 SECONDS TO DECOMPRESSION, the computer said calmly.

Marinos quickly came to a decision and keyed his com. Either the Nikolaos was the biggest lemon in the history of space ship manufacture or those micro-missiles had somehow permitted the enemy to commandeer its core systems. "All crew—abandon ship! Now! Now! Repeat—abandon ship!" *At least the com is working!*

"Come on," Marinos said, leading his men off the bridge. "Get to the pods—and may the gods be kind."

In the main hall of the ship, the walls were lined with single-man escape pods, each capable of sustaining a lost spaceman for years in stasis. Inside the system, it would be a matter of hours before a launch picked them up, but Marinos would be lying if he didn't say he was beyond pissed at losing the *Nikolaos*. She was massively expensive, and only had one year in space—and now this? The Stratocracy would almost certainly demand his suicide, and he wouldn't blame them. This was a failure of unprecedented proportions, and yet he had no idea what he had done wrong… or what he might have done differently.

He jogged into the hall and counted his men as they entered their pods. 14… 15… 16… two more, and he'd jump in himself. The pods popped like champagne corks from the sides of the *Nikolaos* as she neared Owen's gravity. Then with a resonating *CLANG!* the bulkheads slammed shut on either end of the hall. Two men were still missing, Marinos realized. He considering hunting down a pressure suit and reentering the ship to find his men. *ATMOSPHERE VENTED*, came the voice of the ship's AI.

Too late, he thought, cursing as he opened the lid of his pod and jumped into its small padded interior. There was nothing he could do for the missing men now. The lock behind him sealed and he strapped in, then pulled the ejection lever. The system wasn't linked to the main computer system—thank the gods—and the pods still worked. Marinos blessed whatever engineer had designed that failsafe, not that survival would be any better for him than dying with the ship at this point. His death was all but certain either way. *I should go down with* the ship as honor dictates, but I have to tell the Lord Admiral exactly what happened. No one will ever believe it otherwise!

POP! He was off, tumbling into space. A moment later the pod's limited propulsion took over and moved him away from the dark face of Owannis. The pods had proximity detectors which automatically moved them away from gravity wells in case their occupants were incapable of piloting the limited systems on their own. Marinos flipped open the pod's navigation screen and watched as it acquired the moving objects around them. Unlike the sophisticated targeting computers on *Nikolaos*, this was a simple chart of gray objects on a black background. Owannis was easy to spot, as it was the second-largest object on the screen after the planet. Farther off he saw the uneven shape of Stanley, the planet's second moon, almost behind the planet at this point. His pod was a small x in the middle of the screen, and behind it he saw the larger shape of the *Nikolaos* still heading directly towards the face of Owannis.

"Those bastards," he muttered as he looked for the transports that had taken out his ship. There they were—still moving towards the planet. Almost there, in fact.

As he watched, the *Nikolaos* crumpled into the face of Owannis—and a few moments later, the dots of the alien transports vanished into the atmosphere of the planet he had sworn to protect. He cursed them as they disappeared.

It's in the Lord General's hands now, he thought. Gods help the poor bastard!

Ioannes rode on the open deck of a Diosus 50 transport along with the rest of his squad. The Diosus skimmed just above the surface like skating on ice, its antigrav envelope deceptively smooth considering the speed at which they travelled. The report of the *Nikolaos's* shocking demise had been immediately followed by reports of enemy ships entering the atmosphere.

"We're tracking 'em," Overseer Zachaios had announced to his hastily assembled company. "We'll nail them, whoever they are. Infantry units are being activated all over—once we've got a pinpoint on their destination, we'll take them down. Be ready to scramble. Scouts, you're going in first, then call in fire and we'll clean up what's left."

"Probably some religious nuts playing suicide by cop," Orion muttered beside Laedon.

"It must be something of the sort," Laedon said back. "No one would invade an entire planet with nothing more than a pair of transports and some light fighters unless they're suicidal."

"Or they've got better technology," Addams said from Laedon's other side. "Pretty impressive attack so far, taking out *Nikolaos*."

"Total fluke," Orion said. "That ship was too high-tech for its own good. Wouldn't be surprised if that advanced AI went insane under real combat pressure."

"We have a landing," Overseer Zachaios announced, his hand to his ear. "Karabaldi Wilderness Reserve… at least one transport… it's inside our zone… time to move!"

Eight men rode inside the Diosus. It was not an armored transport so they'd be dropped a few kilometers out to cut in on the invader's location and provide intel to the long range artillery already being deployed. The pilot held up two fingers. Two minutes, Laedon thought. He held his PGM-50 close to him and realized his heart was thudding. He hadn't seen any active duty since his state-mandated year of deployment ended seven years ago. Not since before Kaly and the children, he thought.

The Parker slowed behind a rolling ridge of cacti and gorse, not even kicking up dust as it rolled smoothly to a halt. The men jumped to the ground and the Parker returned to base.

"Other side of the ridge, down towards the lake," Orion said, checking his recon tablet. "Looks like we can cut around down the edge of the ridge and follow it closer towards them. There's also a wash cutting through the ridge a bit over a click from here. Team Alpha will cut over on the wash, Beta will continue on to the ridge. Get eyes on them and then we can call in a strike. Watch your optics for scouts."

Grit crunched beneath Laedon's boots as they moved forward. The cover was thin, the plants twisted by lack of rainfall and the burning sun above. Toward the back the woods were thicker, but here there was nowhere to hide. They hit the wash and split with Alpha, moving on towards the ridge. Addams took point, with Laedon, Rollo and Orion behind.

The trees started to thicken as they neared the river and lost a little altitude. Scattered wildflowers started to appear, like blue and yellow eyes watching them pass. Everything was silent except the crunching of their boots and the high buzz of desert cicadas.

"All clear," Addams reported.

"Confirmed, no targets," Orion said.

We'll see them if they're in shooting range, Laedon told himself. We've got the satellites.

He zoomed out on his visor and saw the location of the ship—but there was no troop activity around it. Just the ship. It was as if they were waiting for something. They were only two clicks away on the other side of the ridge.

"We'll be dropping shells on their heads before they manage to get their doors open," Rollo said.

"Almost for certain," Laedon replied, hoping that was the case.

CRACK! A tree exploded behind Rollo—and the man fell to the ground, open-mouthed, a hole burned through his chest.

"DOWN!" Orion yelled.

"I don't see them!" Addams said. "I don't see anything, Sarge!"

"Up there!" Laedon yelled, pointing towards the woods. An armored figure was advancing towards them quickly, rifle in hand. His armor was like nothing Laedon had ever seen. It almost... rippled as he walked, like it was reflecting energy.

"Take him out!" Orion hissed and they opened up, spraying depleted uranium slugs at the enemy. The stranger moved for cover but was knocked to the ground by more than one slug before reaching safety.

"Nailed him," Addams said.

"How did he get so close without our optics letting us know?" Orion said, standing and leaning over Rollo's fallen form. "Dammit," he said, closing their squadmate's open eyes. "All right, let's move in on this guy but don't count on your optics. Trust your eyes. They must be jamming us. For all we know there could be thirty hostiles waiting for us on the other side of the ridge."

The three remaining members of Fire Team Beta moved cautiously towards the man on the ground. As they got closer, Laedon watched the trees for other figures but saw nothing.

"Down and dead as a doornail," Addams reported as they approached the fallen enemy. "We can radio this sucker in."

They looked at the prone figure. His strange armor was pierced in multiple locations. Addams knocked his knuckles on the man's helmet. "Tough stuff," he said. "Not tough enough, though. I wonder where the devil he's from?" he said, turning back to Laedon and Orion with a shrug.

Then the dead man sat up.

"Addams!" Orion yelled—too late!

The invader was up off the ground and firing his rifle in an inhumanly fast flash, spitting accurate blasts of plasma so rapidly that the men couldn't even move their rifles before they were mortally wounded and falling to the ground. Laedon was hit in the side of the neck and the chest. He felt his lungs bubbling and the strangely heady sensation of blood leaving his body.

As he lay bleeding out into the hot sand, the shadow of the enemy stretched over him as the armored invader surveyed his work.

"This is Unternos S696-43V2-4D75-232E. Initial contact," Laedon heard him say in a strangely cold voice. "Four units neutralized. Transmitting location."

Chapter 1

I saw Gunner Naaman Crowe smile as he pulled a slate-blue rifle from a padded case. Our platoon had been called to the range for some special training—and as soon as I saw that smile I knew it was going to be a lot more entertaining than normal. We met in the air-conditioned room inside the big hanger WDI set up as the small arms range. Outside was a serious rifle range with stationary and moving targets, drones and even holographic enemy simulations, but this was more comfortable for talking. And quieter. Even in here, the popping of gunfire outside was loud.

"This, my friends, is Sphinx's latest excursion into the exciting world of long guns," Gunner said, holding up the rifle. "Until last week, it was a classified project. Meet the Sphinx L-24 Fusion-Enhanced Electro-Magnetic Pulse Rifle."

"Also known as the Feemper!" Jones, sitting next to me, announced.

"It's a little too fancy for my taste," Squid muttered from my other side. "New don't mean it's good."

I shot a Sphinx CPB-18 a couple of times on the range. It was a versatile hand-held particle gun, but I never knew Sphinx made rifles.

"You may have heard about this project," Gunner continued. "It's not available in the broader market yet but some of the boys upstairs love us and love their guns, as God intended—so Wardogs is going to be field-testing some of these babies, and although I have no idea who obviously screwed this up, you're the boys who get first crack at it." He paused for a moment. "Try not to break them, if you can manage that."

"Why do we need a fusion-enhanced EMP rifle, I hear some of you thinking," Gunner said. "Are we going to be facing sentient dishwashing machines? Perhaps bust up a tripjacking convention by frying a billion neurons for the price of one? Don't ask me, I'm just your friendly CWO. My job is to introduce you to this lovely lady—where you take her for a date is in the hands of the brass." He stroked the rifle lovingly, then turned to Edgerton who was standing behind him. "Edgerton—you wanna break down the vitals on our new girl, here?"

Edgerton is a thin, balding guy. He's one of those smart nerdlings who will happily run his mouth for hours on anything from antigrav engines to the making of synthetic fabric if you give him half a chance. But his favorite topic is guns, and the smile on his face when Gunner put him front and center told us we were in for an enthusiastic show-and-tell session. At least this one promised to be halfway-interesting.

"Thanks, Gnat," Edgerton said, taking the rifle. "First of all, using this baby on a dishwasher would be a waste."

"How's it work on a fridge?" Jones said.

"Drop the appliances, okay?" Edgerton said, adjusting his glasses. "That would be like using a bulldozer to squash a puppy. So, if I can get back to this bad boy, let me just say the EMP power is similar to a concentrated nuclear blast, capable of overwhelming even the heaviest shielding and toasting electronics like putting a marshmallow into a blast furnace. It's dual-purpose, so if you use the plasma just like your standard issue PN-60s, you can take down anyone wearing armor rated up to 26 KFs. I'll run you through through the wiring specs and the fusion assist—it's really amazing. They fixed the heat issue with a sink that draws it out—I've got the whole thing on my tablet. Actually, yeah, we can jack that into the projector and I'll let you see how they got around the containment issues on the old models. Let me just–"

"That'll do, Edgerton," Gunner broke in. "To summarize, the Sphinx L-24 rips through man and machine alike. And you guys are going to try it out in the field after getting qualified on the range here.

Come on up and grab your guns. I'll get the guys cleared out so we have the place to ourselves."

When I picked up my L-24 I noticed it was heavier than my normal PN-60. That wouldn't matter much in armor. You feel these things without the exo assist, but still—it was nothing like the heavy, ancient slug throwers we carried on the ill-fated Ulixis mission. The blue color was a little flashy for my taste but it wasn't in show-off territory. I wondered if there was any potential for radiation exposure if it was blown up in action but I knew better than to ask Edgerton about it. I wanted to shoot it, not sit through an hour-long lecture on the science of nuclear containment in man-portable devices.

The settings were straightforward enough and Gunner talked us through them with little fuss. On a full-power burst you got 24 shots, then popped in a new charge. Without the full EMP assist, you'd get almost two hundred plasma bolts on a charge. When a charge was used up, an indicator on the bottom flipped red so you didn't pick up a dead one and reload with it. Fresh charges had a green indicator. You get down to a quarter charge and it went yellow. Simple enough. The charges could be reloaded on a proprietary box that plugged into a variety of power outlets, including a solar-powered box with enough efficiency that it could drip-charge under a street light if need be. The charges weren't all that heavy, so you could carry quite a few into combat. Things probably weighed about the same as a golf ball and were about the size of two dominos stuck together. I had to admit, for new tech, it actually appeared to be designed to be battle-friendly.

"We'll start with stationary targets," Gunner said, lining up our platoon in the low tech part of the range where a row of armored plates sat in front of a bank of earth. "Set to plasma just to get the feel. We'll go up to full power later."

I squeezed off a few shots and managed to get a good grouping. The trigger was a little tighter than I liked, but I could get Park to tweak it for me once I was issued one for keeps. I looked down the row and watched as Park put round after round into the dead center of his target. That guy could probably hit flies with rubber bands at fifty feet. Beyond him, Squid was systematically popping off shots. He was holding his own. Despite his initial reticence about the dual-purpose weapon, he looked like he'd been born with an L-24 in his hands.

Next to me, Zelag squeezed off a few rounds, then popped out his charge and looked over the controls on the L-24. He shook his head.

"What is it?" I asked. "You don't like your new toy?"

"No," he said. "It's what it implies about the mission that worries me."

"How so?" I asked.

"Dude," he said. "This isn't just a new toy for Gunner and Edgerton. They're qualifying us on these rifles for a reason."

"Maybe they're phasing out the PN-60?"

"The PN-60 can fire a lot more rounds than these at full power," he said. "And how many times have you ever needed an EMP assist?"

"I dunno," I said. "A few. I usually just use a pulse grenade, though."

"Yeah," he said. "Usually. Unless the enemy isn't human."

"Rogue appliances?" I joked, then had a thought. "Wait a minute, you think we're going up against…"

"The Unity," he said.

"Naw," I said. "Not us. The Ascendancy Marines always deal with them. Or those anti-AI special forces they've got."

"Do they always?" he asked, popping the charge back into his L-24. "I wonder."

"Well, if we end up fighting the Unity, maybe they'll see your cyborged arm and adopt you."

"Screw that," he said, taking a bead on his target. "I'd rather go back to the cannibal zombie death station for dinner than let those freaks mess with my head."

"You're a credit to cyberkind, Zee."

After we got used to firing plasma, Gunner set up Park and released a target drone over the range. Normally, their armor repelled plasma and they'd release a burst of light to let you know when you scored a hit. But when this one flew into range Park nailed the bug-like AI drone with an EMP-assisted blast and that sucker fell from the air like a rock.

I heard Ace whistle. "Nice!" I was glad the lieutenant was in on this training. He was a good pilot but not much of a shot.

"As you can see," Edgerton said, "despite the armor of the target drone, a hit with the EMP assist took it down hard. And it won't fly again, either. It's dead as a doornail. Corporal Park, if you would kindly broaden the EMP range, let's see if we can take out an entire flight at once. Now, we're not going to blow a lot of money here by releasing dozens of drones, but Gunner and I do want you to see the capability this rifle has against AI-driven weaponry. We'll spread them out to simulate a whole swarm coming in."

Edgerton released three drones and they fanned out over the field at about 300 meters range.

"Aim for the center of the swarm and fire when they're within 200," Edgerton instructed. Park adjusted his rifle, aimed, then pulled the trigger. Though the plasma burst hit the center drone, the other two dropped as well—even the one that was more than 50 meters from the one he hit.

"And that's all she wrote!" Zelag said enthusiastically.

"I want to take one of these to a carnival," Jones said. "All those rides, people riding around, then bam! Everything stops!"

"I'd say that was sociopathic, but we've already blown up a science lab and a whorehouse," I told him. "A carnival would kind of complete the set."

"A school would be better," Jones mused.

"See, now that's sociopathic, Tommy," Zelag said, shaking his head.

Gunner and Edgerton set up some terrain drills with drones and we crouched in trenches and took potshots on narrow beam, trying our luck at hitting the rapidly dodging AI drones. "It's important to keep the beam narrow in a combat situation," Gunner explained before we started. "The EMP doesn't care if you hit a robot or your own radio operator—broad spectrum is only useful when you have a clear spot to let loose. It's almost a 180-targeting range, and remember, you can't see it when you fire. Learn to keep them tight, and for Possenti's sake, don't go wrecking your own tech! Tight beam is way more powerful as well, so if the shielding is heavy, keep it tight."

The drones were equipped with heat lasers that stung like the dickens if they managed to nail you—and with their AI targeting and our lack of armor, that happened pretty often. I managed to take one down, so I was pretty proud of myself, but as the last pair of them came in on a run, someone fired, they both dropped, and at the same time, a gagging scream came from somewhere to my right. I heard a shout of "Medic! Medic!" but I couldn't see what happened.

The all-clear sounded and I jumped up from my trench to see what was going on. In the next trench I saw Private Whitter convulsing on the ground. Jock was already there, holding his head and trying to clear his tongue. "He's having a seizure!" he yelled. Another Wardog checked his pulse as Gunner radioed for help. We're all screened for epilepsy, so how was this guy having a seizure?

I watched as they started to give him CPR, pumping his chest and blowing into his mouth. Moments later, a medic arrived from the office and they got Whitter loaded into a biostretcher.

"What happened?" Gunner demanded. "Who hit him?"

"Hit him?" I said. "I don't think anyone shot him."

"Maybe implants?" Edgerton said. "An EMP charge could have screwed up some of his medical implants."

"I think it was my fault, Gunny," Cole said, stepping forward and showing Gunner the settings on his rifle. "I messed up my dispersion. I wasn't anywhere near him, though."

"What part of '180 degrees' did you not understand, Cole?" Gunner snapped, taking the rifle from the man. "Medical implants are computers," he said, addressing all of us. "If you have so much as a bionic appendix, these weapons will mess you up good! We're done with practice for today, but I'm going to expect all of you to put in extra hours on this before I'll qualify you. Especially you, Cole," he said, addressing our hapless squadmate. "So do it, unless you want to end up pushing papers in Corporate while your platoon is out collecting combat bonuses."

Suddenly, those clunky old rifles were looking pretty good by comparison.

Chapter 2

"You suck at darts," Park said, as he sunk his third shot within an inch of the center of the board, completely destroying me for the third game in a row.

"It's never been a priority," I said. "If you weren't a wuss you'd play Zelag instead of me."

"Unfair," Park said, retrieving his darts.

"Yeah, right," I said. "Like you being a sniper ain't."

Park nodded to me. "It is good that you show respect to your betters."

I considered throwing my bottle of *Newt* at the back of his pointy little head but I restrained myself.

"Yo," Jock said, showing up with a dumbbell in each arm, pumping as he walked.

Kantillon HQ had excellent gym facilities, right next door to the game room.

"What's up?" I asked. "You working off a church social?"

"Nailed it," Jock said. "You get the message?"

"Unplugged," I said, tapping the side of my head. "I was tired of getting pinged every time HR changed their laundry policy." We didn't have to stay jacked on base, so I was inside regs.

"Don't disconnect completely—you'll get left out," Jock chided. "Didn't you tell him, Park?" Park shrugged and Jock shook his head. "You're a real team player, Psycho. Anyhow, no problem Tommy. We've got a briefing in an hour. Looks like the Bastards are back in play."

I found myself thinking back to what Zelag had said when we were on the range. It was looking like we'd find out soon if he was right about the Unity.

Marks was expertly shaved and poster-perfect as always, jaw sharp and eyes cold as he surveyed us. "Well, men. We've got a little counter-mercenary work for you."

Interesting, I thought. I wondered which outfit we'd be going up against. Didn't matter, though. We could take anyone in our field. Everyone knows Wardogs has the best and biggest guns for hire.

Marks pulled up a holographic map on the wall of the briefing room, showing a brownish world circled by three moons. He pointed to the planet. "This is Pyrrha. It's a Tech 13 world, so not terribly backwards, but it's nothing to write home about. The larger of the two continents on the surface is dominated by two rival polities, the Demos of Axios and the Sfodrian Stratocracy. They are rivals going back almost to the time of the planet's original colonization, when the first governorship collapsed in a tedious philosophical debate over equality, representation, and the usual academic nonsense. For thousands of years, the two factions drifted apart and went their own ways, neither ever becoming entirely dominant, eventually bringing us to the present. The Axiosi are more liberal in dress and culture, have lots of art and music festivals, engage in a fair amount of manufacturing and interplanetary trade, and are constantly absorbed with all the protests and political parties and orgies and nonsense you'd expect in a democracy. The Sfodrians are more traditionally minded and pride themselves on duty and honor, putting great stock in their history, genealogy, and political unity. They're also one-third the population of Axios, and they're basically an oligarchy ruled by 500 knights, all of whom are extremely accomplished warriors. It's actually one of the craziest military setups you're likely to see."

He clicked a remote and the image in front of us changed to that of a huge mechasuit, its limbs brightly painted and the head decorated with a steel-coated skull. "This here is a Sfodrian knight, wearing his traditional armor. That's something like 18 feet of exo, and the man inside is an absolute master at his craft. The suits are built and maintained by crews of master technicians whose positions are hereditary. These guys are very hard to take down."

"Zelag was wrong," Ward said beside me. "The Feempers gotta be for those dudes."

"They're the crack troops as well as being the leaders of the nation. The other side of the coin is their civilian militia, which is a badly-equipped, poorly-trained mob. The militia has 200,000 members—technically—and they're consistently whipped by the Axiosi. The Axiosi have a professional military of some 30,000 troops, though they get their butts handed to them whenever the Sfodrian knights get involved. So, it's a strange, but stable balance of power."

Ward elbowed me. "Cue the well-compensated imbalancing element."

"You're unbalanced," I told him. He just snorted.

Marks clicked his remote again to show the complete planet hanging in space.

"Recently, the Sfodrians have been having issues with a mercenary force screwing with them. Since Pyrrha does not belong to the Ascendancy, but is a world holding membership in the League of Independent Planets, the TA won't be getting involved in this one."

Big surprise. Everyone wants to be independent until trouble comes knocking.

"These mercenaries managed to take out Sfodria's one planetary defense cruiser a few months back,. Somehow they crashed it into a moon. A new ship, too."

"Sfodrians probably crashed it themselves," Ace muttered from beside me.

"They're losing to these guys," Marks continued. "The mercs are not abiding by any tech level restrictions and they're working with the Axiosi. After losing multiple engagements, Sfodria decided to break open their piggy bank and hire the best in order to hit back hard. That's where you come in. Any questions so far?"

"Yes sir," Squid said in his gravelly smoker's voice. "How big is this merc outfit?"

"We're not sure," Marks admitted.

"Follow-up question," Squid said. "How many of us they paying to send?"

"A platoon," Marks said. There was a rumble of surprise around the room at that. No one was really thrilled with the idea of fighting an unknown number of enemy hostiles with just 24 guys. Especially when said hostiles were backed up by 30,000 pros.

Squid voiced what we were thinking. "You mean to tell me, sir, that we're gonna try and fight an unknown number of advanced-tech bad guys with a single platoon?"

Captain Marks smiled wryly. "Squid, you ought to know me better than that by now. You're not gonna be dropped out there like orphans, without proper support. This is a cadre op, not a combat mission. You're going to be training the Sfodrians and hopefully breaking them of their outdated habits so they can fight more effectively for themselves. You know what they say: Give a man a bodyguard and he's safe for a day. Teach him how to kill everyone else around him and he's safe for life. That said, the Sfodrian knights are some serious fighters, and they've been getting killed by these mercs. Twenty-five have been lost at last report and that's absolutely unprecedented in their history. So, you are going in and you're going to figure out how they're losing, why they're losing, and how to stop doing it."

Marks clicked his remote and brought up an image of a knight in a field. His highly decorated armor was blackened with soot but looked otherwise unharmed. "Here, watch this encounter."

The image began to move. It appeared to be captured via drone from above the knight. There was some plasma fire from a scrubby patch of brown woods and cacti. The knight rolled into a ball and rocketed towards the source of the fire at some 80 clicks per hour, tearing a rut and kicking up a cloud of dust as he moved. The plasma fire splattered off his armor without effect as he barreled up to the edge of the brush, then stood upright and brandished a pair of glowing energy swords, swinging them through the vegetation like butter as he moved in towards the enemy position.

"Can you believe this guy?" Jones said. "This is better than the last movie I saw since… ever!"

"That's freaking intense," Ward said.

A shell or a grenade blast burst in front of the knight, knocking him backwards. He snapped back up quickly, crouching and releasing a stream of pulsing energy blasts from his swords.

"What the devil, will you look at that?" someone said behind me, whistling at the improbable attack.

"I want one," Zelag said, mostly to himself.

The fire from the woods came to a halt—but then another shell exploded from behind the knight, knocking him to the ground again. He recovered and spun about, unleashing more plasma, but then the camera blurred and moved out, showing multiple squads and artillery closing in on the man's position.

"Why is this guy alone?" Ward muttered, watching as plasma and shells zipped in from multiple angles. It was hard to see with all the dust the fire was kicking up, but like ants swarming over a lizard, the Axiosi troops finally stopped the warrior, pinning him down under a relentless barrage until his armor failed and he was finally blown to pieces by incoming mortar shells.

We clapped, slowly, somberly, but respectfully. The man died well, and he took more than a few of his enemies with him.

"And there you have an example of their best warriors," Marks said as the screen went black. "They're good, but they're not good enough. As you can see, the guy was alone—and they often fight alone. Sure, they'll go out in a group when they have to, but they're all on their own out there in the field. This guy got in over his head. Even with that, he apparently took out over a hundred troops, a couple of jeeps and a tank before they finally nailed him. Like I said, they're good—and the armor is awesome. They just need some better tactics."

He clicked his remote and switched the screen to another video. "Now let's take a look at one of the mercs we'll be facing."

The footage rolled and I saw about a platoon of guys outside the walls of what looked like a power plant. The video was somewhat grainy and seemed to be a security camera capture from on top of a pole or something.

"These are some of the Sfodrian National Militia," Marks narrated. "They were called out of the city after a report of a landing by an unknown craft. Keep your eyes to the right—in just a moment…"

There was a flash of light and a couple of men fell, causing the rest of the platoon to hit the ground. I couldn't see the source of the fire thanks to the camera angle, but more came in with deadly rapidity, sweeping over the troops on the ground as they fired back with their rifles. One by one, all of them were taken out—and then something blurry moved into the frame through the fallen forms, distorting the bodies as it passed.

"Gotta be a cloaked suit," Ward said quietly. "And some solid armor, too. I wonder where the rest of that guy's squad is, though."

"That's it," Marks said, answering Ward's question. "One guy."

On screen, the blur figure turned solid, revealing a black form in a battlesuit.

"That's an Axiosi uniform, by the way. You'd never know he was anything else," Marks said.

The man was carrying a bag from which he pulled multiple objects and attached them to the wall of the power station. He walked away—and about a minute later, the screen exploded into white static.

"One guy," Marks said. "Took out the platoon, then blew the power station. Thoughts?"

"Yes," Zelag spoke up. "This guy was slick. Obviously, the local troops weren't ready for him and weren't well-trained, but still, that's not some pirate merc working off his gambling debts."

"Yeah," Jock said. "That camo suit probably cost more than a tank."

"Agreed," Marks said. "It's got to be a serious operation. And their use of high tech is why we had you guys training on the Sphinxes. Fight fire with fire, and tech with tech. Another thing to keep in mind is that they seem to be training the locals too. That first video you saw where the Axiosi took down a Sfodrian knight, those tactics were new, according to our clients. They're learning to coordinate their assaults and take the initiative, rather than just heading for the hills whenever a knight appears.

"Unless anyone has a serious aversion to this mission and would rather be reassigned to janitorial duties, we've chosen you Bastards to go. I'll brief Squid on your travel arrangements and he'll take care of the rest. Any more questions?"

"Yes sir," Jock said. "We really don't have any idea at all who these mercs are, not even any rumors about rivals that might be operating in the area?"

"No idea," Marks said. "They come in, hit a few things, leave, then come back again."

"Could it be the Unity, sir?" Ward asked.

"That's what you're going to find out for us. Dismissed."

Park munched on something that looked like a tumorous kidney as a group of us ate lunch in the cafeteria. Beside him, Zelag swallowed a slug of green liquid and shuddered, then pushed the glass away and tucked into a salad.

"What is that stuff you're drinking?" I asked Zelag, as I took a bite of my cheesesteak sandwich.

"Kale juice," he said. "Blame Jock."

Park shook his head. "Some people have no tastebuds."

I laughed, looking at Park's disgusting meal. "Dude, you're not one to talk about tastebuds."

"Just like Mom used to make it," Park said, slurping a forkful of wormlike strings in brown liquid.

"This looks like an interesting assignment," Zelag said, changing the subject. "I'm telling you, it's gotta be the Unity."

"I dunno," I said. "I don't know much about them, but I doubt they'd be interested playing mercs for some petty world in the League. What do they care about money? It's probably just a new corporate outfit."

"Maybe they're a gazillionaire's new toy," Park said. "The Unity hunts bigger game than some pissant war on a nothing planet."

Zelag shrugged as he crunched on a crouton. "I hope so. I liked those guys with their huge servo-mechs, though. I saw a documentary on them once. They have these ancestral houses that custom-design the mechs, and the pilots have all kinds of honor codes and rules. Twenty of them once took an entire island of 100,000 people and made it a vassal state. Twenty! Can you believe that?"

"It looks cool enough, but it's kind of stupid," Jones said from behind me. He sat at the table with a plate of steak and potatoes. "If they didn't blow all their resources on turning their nobles into one-man wrecking balls, they might actually have cash to fund a decent military." He sawed off a chunk of steak and chewed it, talking around his mouthful of meat. "Looks like the regulars can't fight their way out of a plastic bag."

"I wouldn't mind one of those plasma swords," I admitted. "They were awesome."

"Sure," Park said. "Until you get pinned down at range."

"They're like the samurai," Zelag said. We looked at him blankly. "Oh, come on," he said. "Old Earth tribe called the Japaneesi. Super-sharp swords, lots of honor and tradition, just like the Sfodrians."

"Honor won't save you from artillery," Jones said. "That's why our motto is 'off the chain', not 'be stupid and die following the stupid rules.'"

"They didn't believe that way," Zelag said. "In fact, they say an army of them attacked an emplacement of machine guns armed with nothing but their family swords."

"What happened?" Park said.

"They all died," Zelag confirmed my suspicions.

"Great story, Z," Jones said. "See, that's exactly what I'm talking about."

"So we'll bring these guys into the 31st century," I said. "Even some basic squad tactics would go a long way towards making them a first-class fighting force. They have the courage to burn, obviously. Morale, initiative, they've got everything you need for an elite unit."

"And we need to train some sense into their regulars," Zelag said. "They're worse than cannon fodder now. Everything depends on those ancient knights with their blinged-out super-armor; meanwhile, the grunts get mowed down by a single merc in a camo suit."

"Yeah," Jones agreed. "Stupid."

"Well, we better figure out how to make them less stupid," I said, licking the grease off my fingers and grabbing my tray to leave. "I'm gonna pack up. See you at the briefing."

Chapter 3

Squid told us that since we were only a platoon, Captain Marks had decided to send us via commercial liner instead of contracting a ship for us. That meant we had to find our civvie IDs and ditch all our guns and goodies, then dress like normal people. No gun-brand shirts, either, was the word from on high. That narrowed my choices—but it completely eliminated all of Zelag's wardrobe. I ended up lending him a few of my shirts. We were assured, promised, and guaranteed that our weapons and gear would be sent safely on a separate transport. That elicited dubious groans all around. We all remembered Ulixis.

"I better not end up carting some crappy local rifle around in my long underwear," Jones complained.

"You have long underwear?" I asked, but he was too busy trying to jam a game console into his carry-on pack to answer.

At 0500 our platoon stood in the cold morning air waiting for our transport to arrive at base, looking like the fittest, toughest, most technologically-enhanced group of civilians that ever walked the planet.

"These are for you boys to wear now and again on your flight," Squid said, walking out with a couple of bags from which he withdrew matching purple shirts. "It's part of your cover. You all are now fitness coaches working with a very respectable non-profit organization that didn't exist until an hour ago."

I held up the shirt he'd given me. On the left chest was a logo of a bicep containing a galaxy and the words "Team Galaxy Fitness!" in irritating letters that were apparently supposed to be funny.

"Don't talk too much," Squid continued, "but if you're asked about what you do, you're all really interested in teaching troubled youth the transformative power of active living."

"The what power?" Ward looked puzzled.

"Troubled high school girls!" Jones looked pleased.

Squid turned to him and cocked an eyebrow. "When I said, 'Don't talk too much,' I should have said 'except for Jones.' Jonesy, you don't talk at all. To anyone. As for the rest of you, just be cool. We're going incognito, but don't let down your guard and don't think this is a joke. We have no idea who we're facing yet, so we don't know how good their corporate spies are. We're gonna be friendly but non-talkative, we're gonna act like civilians, we're not gonna push people around, we're not going to get in any fights, and we're gonna keep our eyes open. Clear?"

Squid tossed his now-empty bags into a recycler chute and lit up a cigar. After a few puffs, he spoke again. "Almost forgot to tell you. Whitter made it and he's out of medical. The medics kept him alive long enough for the docs to get his implants straightened out. He's not approved for duty yet, but he's gonna be fine."

A sigh of relief and approval swept through the group. Risking life and limb is part and parcel of being a mercenary, but somehow, it's worse when you lose a man to something stupid and unnecessary. We once had a guy killed by a crate that fell out of a transport as we were offloading for a mission. Dead is dead, but still, there are worse ways to go than dying in battle. No one wants to be remembered as a joke, or worse, a screwup.

Everyone but Zelag put on the new purple shirts in the transport on the way to Ergman Memorial Spaceport. The ocular reader scanned our irises at the gate to confirm our reservations, we worked our way through the security line, and eventually boarded the Terran Space-ways liner *Gondola*.

Gondola was one of those not-quite-a-cruise-ship ships that had decent cabins, simple rec facilities, a pair of bars and a round-the-clock cafeteria. Compared to a typical Wardogs transport, it was high-class passage. We did split rooms, though, as WDI's accountants weren't enthusiastic about wasting money on personal comfort.

Forward held the typical row seating where all passengers were belted in for takeoff before being released to the rest of the ship once we exited atmo. We scattered through the crowd in search of our seats. I ended up in between a opiate-thin syntar musician and a sour-faced old guy who looked like he lived on vinegar and aspirin.

"Hey," the old guy said, trying to pack his carry-on into the overhead bin for takeoff. "Your syntar is taking up too much space."

"Just be glad I don't play the organ," the musician laughed. The old guy's eyes narrowed and he looked like he was going to punch the younger man.

"I fail to see the humor in this situation!" he snapped back.

"The musician's union made a deal to consider syntars legitimate carry-on, sir," the musician said, making the "sir" sound like a curse.

"Oh yeah?" the man said. I could see he was about to launch into what promised to be an epic tirade.

"Hey!" I broke in, taking the old guy's arm in my right hand and grabbing the musician's arm in my left, then gave them both a little pressure on the nerves. "Let's just be cool, okay? It's a long flight and I didn't pay to sit and listen to you two bitch at each other." I smiled and squeezed just a little harder. Both looked at me and decided to end their argument. It felt good bringing peace and order to the universe.

We spent two days on *Gondola*, then jumped and spent another day in transit to Feymanus, where we landed at Pallas International Spaceport for a four-hour layover. That's where I cracked a guy's skull open. So much for universal peace.

I'd been sitting in a cafe in the outer rim of the spaceport, about ten gates from where we were going to pick up our ship for the next leg of the trip. Our ultimate destination was the Dom Sevru system, but we had to go through Feymanus, then jump through to Rhysalan, then to Terentulus, over to Merovinge and up through Mosva. Like Park said, it was a pissant planet. Just look up the sector map—you'll see what I mean. Anyhow, I was sitting outside this cafe, eating a stale pastry and drinking a coffee that wasn't quite as terrible as I expected, when this guy caught my eye in a bad way. You know how it is when you just feel that someone is off. It's usually in the eyes, and you can sense it once you've dealt with enough bad guys. But I've learned to trust my gut over the years, and this thick guy with fleshy lips and a razor-stubbled head was triggering my radar.

He was sitting there poking around on a little tablet, pretending not to be watching Cole and Waterose where they sat at a table inside the cafe. I keyed my com jack to Ward's channel. "Ward, it's Falkland. Come to the cafe in Sector 18," I said, glancing up at the signage. "Be cool and ignore the guys inside. I'm at the outside table."

"Roger," he replied. "Be there in five."

Before he arrived, the thick guy got up and walked past Cole and Waterose, glancing at them again as he passed. He stepped out into the concourse and started walking towards the rest rooms. Once I was sure of his destination, I relaxed. Ward showed up a moment later and I swigged my coffee and chucked the rest of the inedible pastry into a chute. "Ward—I think we got a spook. He was eyeing the boys over there."

"Where is he now?" Ward said, looking around.

"Restrooms. Let's corner him."

"You got it," he said. "Want to let Cole and Waterose know?"

I looked over at the two of them, engrossed in a gun site they'd pulled up on the table display. "Nah, you and me are better at this. Change your shirt," I said, pointing to his purple polo. I was already wearing a regular T-shirt. Ward nodded and pulled a less conspicuous shirt out of his backpack.

We headed to the restroom and stepped inside. Our target was in a stall and another guy was washing his hands. In the corner was a utility closet. I opened it like I belonged there and pulled out a mop, a bucket and a "CAUTION" cone, then nodded to the guy who was now drying his hands. When he left I splashed water all over the floor outside the entrance and put up the cone, then wedged the door shut with the mop. Ward grinned at me, then knocked on the stall door. "Hey buddy, you gonna be in there all day?" he said.

"What's your problem?" came an angry voice, followed by the sound of the toilet's incinerator turning on.

"Cleanup crew," Ward said. "Come out of there."

The door latch clicked and the door opened slightly. Ward pulled it open, then came flying backwards as the man caught him unexpectedly with a hard punch to the face. Ward staggered backward, blood welling from a split lip. "You bastard," he yelled, spitting blood. As the guy exited the stall, I saw he had an object clenched in his fist. He'd hit Ward with something.

"Back off!" he snarled at us and making a move for the main door.

"Stand down," I said, blocking him. "You're a little on edge for a civilian, aren't you?"

"Screw you," he said, trying to shove past me. Ward grabbed his shoulder and nailed him in the side of the head with his fist, knocking him into the doorjamb. The guy thrashed about but I hit him in the stomach with a rear hand, doubling him over.

"I saw you watching my men," I hissed. "Who are you working for?"

The guy grabbed at one of my legs and punched upwards into my crotch. It was only a glancing blow, so it didn't slow me down any, but it did infuriate me. I grabbed behind his head and kneed him hard in the face, then pulled him into another rear hand that knocked him out on his feet. He collapsed backwards onto the tile and hit so hard I heard his skull crack. He jerked and twitched for a second, then lay still. Blood began to spill from the back of his head.

"Geez, Tommy, I think you killed him," Ward said.

"You think?" I said, a little surprised. I leaned in and put my hand on his neck. At first his pulse was pumping like a machine gun but as I felt his throat, it slowed down, and came to a full stop.

"He pissed me off. And it isn't like we had the time or the space to interrogate him properly." I pried open the dead man's fingers to see what had cut Ward's lip. It was small metal cylinder. I looked at it close. It was some sort of recording device. Ward went to the sink and washed out his mouth, then dabbed some wet paper towels on the bleeding cut. When he was done fixing his face, I handed him the cylinder. "What do you think?"

"Probably a full-spectrum environmental recorder. Audio, video, etc. Holographic capture. Looks like you made him right."

"Good thing, too," I said. "Considering I killed him and all that."

"Yeah," Ward said, going over to take a look at the dead man. "I'll take pics with my retinal cam and we'll see if we can dig up any details on him."

"Get a chunk of something for a DNA scan, too." I said.

The restroom door rattled and I heard an irritated voice outside.

"Let's stick him back in the stall," I said. Ward got his shots and took a wad of hair—I didn't ask from where—then we wrestled him up onto the toilet and sat him up on it, slumped against the side of the stall. I locked the door from the inside and crawled out underneath. Ward was already mopping up the blood on the tiles. The restroom door rattled again.

"Just hold on," I yelled. I looked at Ward's bloody lip and realized that I didn't have any fuseglue or anything to stick it together. "Better just keep the paper towels on it," I said. Ward nodded and threw out the first blood-soaked wad and grabbed some fresh ones. I opened the door to discover a line of three waiting outside.

"Hey, buddy—what's the deal?" an older guy in a suit said as he stepped in, followed by a younger man in a Jonny Torqueband T-shirt and a 12-year old kid. A line had obviously been forming. "This is a public restroom."

"Apologies," I said, putting my arm around Ward's shoulders. "Air-port security. This gentleman here had an accident and we didn't want to alarm anyone."

"Whoa," said the guy in the T-shirt. "Looks like he needs a medic."

"I think you're right," I said, walking out. "Thank you for your patience."

We walked quickly back to our gate where I found Squid waiting for us.

"What the hell?" he muttered as we walked up. "A spontaneous dojo break out at the cafe?"

"You got something to stop the bleeding?" He nodded and rifled through his carry-on case.

Jock raised his eyebrows at me.

"It's nothing," I said, knowing that spaceport security was probably recording everything that happened. "Ward slipped and fell. We took care of it."

"Terran Spaceways *Gondola* will be departing the system in 2 kiloseconds," announced the spaceport speakers. "Passengers are advised to board now and prepare for launch."

Squid put his hand on my arm. "You and Ward better sit next to me."

Over the first ten minutes of our voyage, Ward and I quietly provided a verbal After-Action Report to Squid in between the mandatory safety lectures from the crew. "You sure he was a spy?" he said. "Recorder doesn't prove anything. Maybe he was a journalist. Or maybe he wasn't even spying on us."

"I've got face shots and DNA samples," Ward said. "Any way we can scan them and send them on?"

"Hmm," Squid said. "Maybe." He thought for a moment. "Edgerton is with us. He's a smart cookie. Has an augment, too."

"Yeah, he might have an idea."

"Worth trying," Squid said. "Though I wish we were on one of our ships right now and had access to the proper gear. This civilian smokescreen is a pain in the ass." He gnawed at his lip. "Not only don't we have our digitals, the damn stewardesses won't let me smoke."

When we exited atmo and were released from our seats Ward and I found Edgerton sitting in the lounge area, staring off into space, communing with the AI gods.

"Sergeant Edgerton?" I said. He didn't say anything so I kicked his foot.

"Falkland," he said, blinking a few times. "Were you and Mr. Ward having differences of opinion earlier?"

"We were on the same page, actually," I told him. "Is your augment capable of forensics? DNA?"

"Sure, within certain limits," he said. "Babbage is capable of the basic scans, provided it's human. Can't deal with all the exobiological sequencing unless I purchase a module for him." He paused for a moment. "Yeah, he really wants that module, I don't know why. He's an info-junkie. You could download a bazillion terabytes on sea snails and he'd eat it up—it's not about the info, it's just the–"

"Great," Ward said, his voice thick around his swollen lip. "We need Babbage to help us nail down the guy that gave me this lip. Squid said you could probably help."

"You don't know who hit you?"

"No," Ward said. "I saw who hit me before Tommy taught him some manners. But we need an ID. Look into my ocular implant and I'll pass the images to Babbage." Edgerton did, then blinked a couple of times.

"Ugly guy," he said. "Babbage isn't hooked up to our database, though, so he has no idea who this is."

"Listen, Sarge," I said. "Babbage just needs to get the data to the subsector HQ on Rhysalan and have them run the pics. We don't expect him to work it out on his own."

"Also, scan this and get the DNA," Ward said, producing a paper towel-wrapped clump of hairs from his pocket. "Send it on."

"Hmm, that takes some thought," Edgerton said. "Oh, yes. Here's a good idea. Maybe I could hack the next messenger drone the ship sends on ahead. It would simply take one access node, and once I'd corrupted that, I'd just have to–"

"Thanks, Edgerton," I said, cutting him off. "I'm sure you've got it under control."

"So what happened with Ward?" Zelag asked. We were splitting a cabin for this leg of the flight.

"So you just got a bad feeling and decided to call Ward?" Zelag said after I filled him in. "Then decided it was confirmed by the fact the guy punched someone trying to accost him in a bathroom stall?" He rolled a small medallion back and forth over his metal fingers thoughtfully. "Risky, but I'd say that was a good read, Tommy. You should have worked diplomatic security."

"Did you miss the part where I cracked his skull?"

"Yeah, they do tend to frown on that, actually."

I shrugged. "I don't think the guy was a real pro. It was more than obvious he was keeping an eye on the boys, although he missed me. He could have just recorded everyone quietly and reviewed the tapes at his leisure. The recorder we took wasn't cheap. It would've done the job."

"It doesn't take a genius to blow up a ship, though," Zelag said, setting the medallion on the desk.

"What?" I said. "Who said anything about blowing up ships?"

"Dude, you wouldn't believe some of the nonsense that took place when I was working diplomacy. Remember that CEO who got poisoned right in front of us? That sort of stuff happens more than you'd think. It can get even weirder. We once caught ourselves a dwarf assassin climbing through an air duct on his way to slit the throat of a Valatestan executive."

"A dwarf?"

"Yeah, an actual dwarf. Genetically modified. He was small enough to fit through the ducts. They didn't count on the microfilter installed above the office, though. He was trying to saw through it when the MPs caught him."

"So you're saying this guy could have been doing more than just gathering info?"

"Sure," he said, picking up the medallion again and spinning it on the table. "It'll be interesting to see what comes back from Rhysalan HQ, if anything. Better to be paranoid than dead."

"Yeah," I said, watching the medallion spin to a rattling halt on the table. "Agreed."

Throughout the two-day journey to Rhysalan I kept my eyes open but didn't see anyone else who looked suspicious. The passengers were your typical lot. A few aliens, a lot of business people, some families visiting relatives, retirees seeking some excitement in a new system, a few boys from the TA Navy going home to see family, but there was no one that hit me as off, not that I'm some sort of psychic or anything. Squid had passed the word to the other guys to keep their eyes open but we got nothing. Edgerton even hacked the manifest and we pored through it but found nothing interesting.

We docked at Port International outside Rhysalan for a 24-hour re-fueling and maintenance layover. Two hours before we were supposed to board for the next leg, Squid received a message from the surface and called us in to a private conference room.

"Well boys," he said, puffing on an e-cigar he'd gotten from some-where, "we've got some interesting news from the intel guys on the surface."

The faces around the table were attentive.

"I clued you in on Tommy and Ward's little bathroom incident already. Turns out Falkland was right. The gentlemen in question was indeed an intelligence agent."

"Whose?" Jock asked.

"Axios. The opfor on Dom Servru. It took longer than expected to run him down since he'd had some facial surgery, but the DNA clinched it. They managed to pull up an old file from a TA list of known corporate spies. He was kicked off Faraday at one point for an unauthorized archive access, then went dark for a while. Later turned up on Pyrrha. Apparently, the Axiosi government caught word that we were on our way to help out their rivals."

"So they were tracking us," Zelag said. "For what purpose?"

"Maybe just eyes on the ground," Park said.

"Maybe," Squid said, exhaling a cloud of vapor that smelled like the animal skin leather they sell on colony worlds.

"We should cancel the next leg," I said.

"What?" Jock said. "You kidding? Can the mission?"

"No," I said. "Of course not. But I've been talking with Zelag. He thinks they might be trying to head us off."

"Talk to me," Squid said, looking at Zelag.

"Well," Zelag said, tapping his fingers on the table. "I was thinking that they were just looking to confirm who we were so they can hit the right ship."

"Hit?" Jock said.

"Yeah," Zelag said. "Hit. As in, take us out before we reach our destination."

"Seriously?" Ace chimed in. "Taking out a commercial liner full of people just to kill 24 Wardogs?"

"Wardogs put the fear of God into people," Edgerton said.

"Yeah," Jones said, "but so do Starkillian bat spiders. I'm with Ace on this one. You'd have to be nuts or desperate to take out a ship full of civilians."

"No, just ruthless," Zelag said. "Trust me. I've seen crazier stuff than this. There's a low-level war going on here. Acceptable losses are part and parcel of interstellar diplomacy. Besides, losing a ship in deep space in transit between systems can be explained away. No witnesses if it's total."

"Geez," Cole said.

Multiple Wardogs were shaking their heads. I could see Zelag's idea wasn't flying.

"Paranoid," Jones said. "That's totally paranoid."

"How hard is it to just cancel our tickets and take another ship?" I asked. "Seriously, why not do it?"

"Accounting will throw a fit, for one," Squid said.

"So what?" Zelag said. "There's maintenance work happening on *Gondola* right now. You think it would be hard to pay off some mechanic with a few debts and get inside and do a little screwing around with life support—or the reactor core? I'd say we pushed our luck already by taking this last leg after finding a spy."

"Sure, it would be possible to do. But it's a civilian ship," Jones said.

"Yeah, these amateurs don't scare me," Ward said. "They may scare Tommy and Cyborg here, but I say we stick with the program. Time is wasting."

Squid puffed his fake stogie as we pushed back and forth, arguing over the risks and calling each other names. After a few minutes, he rapped his knuckles on the table. "All right, that's enough," he growled. "We'll switch ships and take another flight so Tommy and Zelag can get some sleep."

"What?" multiple voices burst out, most of them sounding irritated.

"You gotta be kidding!" Jones yelled.

"No," Squid said. "Tommy was right about the spy, plus Zelag has made his point in my head. It's only a few thousand credits to cash out our tickets and buy replacements. If the delay is less than a few days, it won't harm the mission any. HQ will pony up. It may be a slight risk, but it's a risk and it's unnecessary. So we won't take it."

"But–" Jones said.

"No more," Squid said, standing. "This discussion is over. We'll take another ship to Terentulus."

Ten hours later we boarded the *Concordia II*, a budget system-hopper that only serviced the Rhysalan-Terentulus route. The seats were uncomfortable and the coffee was bad. Multiple Wardogs bitched me and Zelag out over the cut-rate accommodations, but we made it to Terentulus without mishap. As we waited in the spaceport for Squid to finalize our tickets on the next ship, a few of us sat on a bench watching ships come and go, trying to name the manufacturers. I had a thought and nudged Edgerton awake. "Sarge, wake up," I said.

"Tommy? What's up?" he said, blinking and trying not to yawn in my face.

"Hey, is your augment hooked into the station net?"

"Of course," he confirmed.

"Can you look up *Gondola*."

Jones leaned in. "Please tell us she made it here a day ago so we can all mock Tommy and Cyborg."

Edgerton's eyes unfocused, then refocused a few moments later. "No way," he said. "No way…"

"What?" Jones asked.

"She didn't… it never…"

"*Gondola* didn't make it here?" Ward asked, looking up from a wrap he was demolishing.

Edgerton shook his head. "She never showed up. The notice says her arrival is 'delayed' and Terran Spaceways has launched an inquest. A request has been submitted to the TA and two system navies for a rescue ship. There are lots of families posting requests for news about missing family members, too. Babbage is going through the news now. Possible pirates, maybe systems failure, no wreckage or black box found yet. Last known location was before the jump point out of Rhysalan."

"Whoa," Jones said. "You don't think…" He trailed off, then cursed.

I was shocked. It's one thing to play it careful, but it's another to discover that you're not paranoid, they really are out to get you. I have to admit, I almost didn't back up Zelag on the change of transport. Damn good thing I did, though.

"That means Zelag was right," Ward commented. "I mean, about the Unity."

"How do you figure that?"

Ward paused and stared at his wrap reflectively for a moment. When he looked up at me, his eyes were dark with foreboding.

"Because they're not human anymore. They don't give a damn about human life and they damn sure don't fuck around."

Chapter 4

Pyrrha looks pretty rough from the sky. It's full of mountains, ridges, and rocks, cities scattered about the valleys, lots of dry, brown terrain with some green areas around lakes.

I had done my research and learned that the Dom Sevru system has two habitable planets, Epimetheus, the first planet, and Pyrrha with its two moons. Due to its toxic atmosphere and extreme temperature, Epimetheus is mostly unpopulated except for some mining colonies and the techs at a huge solar array that beam-powered cargo transports. Prometheus, the dark red sun around which our beleaguered clients orbited, was a real scorcher. We were informed that the UV load on Pyrrha, though nothing like that of Epimetheus, meant going outside for more than a few minutes without sunscreen wasn't advisable. The locals had a UV-blocking gene sequence that went back to the original colonists but we Wardogs weren't going to be catching rays on the surface.

Of course, we would probably be in our battlesuits anyhow, so it was hardly a problem.

We disembarked from the *Concordia II* at the small Sfodrian orbital spaceport and took a lander down to the capital city of Nepolon, the so-called City of Lords that was known as the ancestral meeting place of the Five Hundred. Who now, apparently, were more accurately described as the Four Hundred Seventy Five. We didn't land in Nepolon as I thought we would, but coasted another 40 clicks past the city to a fortified base surrounded by shooting ranges on one side and a town on the other. There was a parking area with some aged military transports, a broadcast tower, water and fuel storage tanks and a generator building, rows of barracks, a big hangar with a WDI flag hanging over the front next to a local flag.

Outside the base was a severe little company town of maybe five thousand people. Everything was straight, clean lines and right angles. The place was too sharp, severe, orderly, organized and too stripped down to look welcoming, but to my eye, it indicated something even better. It indicated competence.

"Welcome to Pyrrha, boys," we heard an unexpectedly cheerful voice as we stepped off the lander and blinked in the hot red sun. I looked to see a broad-shouldered guy in his fifties with a big mustache, wearing a floppy campaign hat. "Come on in the hanger. I've already got your stuff all squared away."

I liked him already. Zelag was so relieved, he looked like a man on death row given a reprieve.

"Garvin Pitt," Squid said with a grin, slapping the man on the back. "So this is where you ended up. You're our logistics?"

"Yes indeed, Lieutenant!" Pitt said, pumping Squid's hand. "Short-term gig, kind of surprised I took it myself. But it's not bad. Sfodria is a serious little place, but I like the order of it all. No one spits on the sidewalk here and there isn't any litter or graffiti to be seen anywhere." He looked at Cole's purple polo shirt, then around at a few other guys who were wearing theirs as well. "Team Galaxy Fitness? This some sort of new division or something?"

"The brass's idea of sneaking about. It didn't work," Squid said, pulling a cigar from his shirt pocket. "Never mind that. You really got our stuff?"

"Of course," Pitt said, waving towards a big mess of assorted containers. "Who's got your back, buddy?"

"All of our stuff?" Squid pressed, lighting his smoke.

"Armor, rifles, frags, everything on the manifest. Hixton Freight dropped it off a day ago. They're doing better than Upperfield.

Though that doesn't take much. Upperfield once sent a pair of our pulse howitzers to a daycare center–"

"What the hell?" Squid said.

"On the wrong planet too. But I'll bet the kiddies were all excited with their funny new teeter totters. Hey, before we get started, why don't you guys help yourself to what's in the cooler there," he gestured to a silver cooler on the ground by one of the buses. "Local brew isn't bad, once you get used to it."

"Took me a whole week to figure out they'd gotten our howitzers," Pitt continued, sitting down on a bench. "I was too busy trying to figure out who had sent all the rainbow-colored child-size chairs. UF's tracking system is a clusterfutastrophe." He cracked open a strange green can and laughed. "So hey, tell me about your life. Lungs are good, obviously."

"No rejection issues since they're artificial," Squid said, blowing a fat smoke ring in the still air of the hangar. "Still feel a little weird in my ribs sometimes. I think they inflate a little farther than my old set."

"No doubt," Pitt said. "Hey, you weren't in on that Ulixis thing were you?"

"No, dammit," Squid said. "Tech restrictions."

"We don't have to worry much about those here," Pitt said, taking a slug of his drink. "TA regulations don't apply and the League doesn't even try to interfere. What specifically kept you from going, though?"

"No implants allowed. Not even medically approved ones."

"Strict," Pitt commented. "So I guess you weren't there for the famous incident everyone was talking about?"

"Incident?"

"You know, the thing with Marks!"

"Ask Park or Tommy or Jock here. Actually, about half these guys were there, I think."

Pitt turned to me. "So, is it true?"

"Is what true?" I said.

He leaned forward in a conspiratorial manner. "Did Captain Marks really glass an entire city to take out a royal family?

I shrugged. "Nuclear technology was not prohibited…."

"I knew it!" he said triumphantly. "You know, I heard he once rammed a big shipping transport with a space-to-ground lander because they wouldn't move out of the way. Put a gun to the captain's head, told him to crank up the shields and goose the engines. Blew a hole right through the middle!"

"Really?" I said, not believing a word of it. I wasn't an expert on ship architecture, but it sounded highly improbable.

"Total truth," Pitt said. "Guy I served with heard it from a lieutenant whose brother was on the ship. Marks's ship, that is, not the one he wrecked. The man is a legend!" He turned to the rest of us. "Hey, you guys want something to eat? I think we could scrounge up some edibles in the office if you give me a hectasec or two."

"Go for it," Squid said. "Team Galaxy Fitness is devoutly committed to proper nutrition."

Pitt whistled to a couple of local contractors unpacking a container. "These men need food, so go out and grab whatever you can find. And put on some coffee from my private stash." The men nodded and disappeared.

"You got a schedule for us yet?" Squid asked.

"Actually, yeah," Pitt said, pulling out a chunky old Spekker all-weather field tablet. "Off to our private barracks—which is really a motel just on the other side of the road past the base fence, we just rented the whole thing out—and then you've got an appointment with Captain Herevos and Lord General Landros at 1600."

"I have no idea what time it is now," Squid said. "We need to sync to local. Should have done it on the transport."

"It's 1190. A day is just shy of 76 kilosecs here. They use hours, each about three kaysecs. You can sync to Jimbo in the office there if you scan in, he'll reset you."

"Jimbo?"

"AI in a box. Over twenty years old but he's good on tracking stuff for me. More stable than the emo-enhanced models coming out these days."

"Stay with what works," Squid said, blowing a smoke ring. "I keep telling people that. What's the situation on the ground here?"

"I can fill you all in with what I know. It's not pretty."

"Men, Pitt here's gonna give us a briefing," Squid said, calling in those of us that were farther away. "Come on over."

We gathered around and Pitt laid out the local situation.

"Sfodria is really in a bind," Pitt said. "Axios has never been able to whip them like they're getting whipped now. It's the mercenaries; they are taking out the knights, and that is unthinkable. No one's ever knocked out more than one or two in the past, and we're up to twenty-seven down now. Lost another two this week."

"So who are the mercs?" Zelag asked.

Pitt shrugged and threw his empty drink can towards a trash chute, missing completely. "No outfit we ever dealt with before. We know almost nothing but I've been able to surmise a few things. Cloaking tech, good weapons, and man, they're seriously bold. They came in with these little ships, right past the cruiser— I'm sure you heard about that, they smashed it into Owannis— then the militia responds and they take 'em out like nothing, then they meld right into the Axiosi infantry like they was born to it. Since then, the combined Axiosi and mercs have nailed the Sfodrian militia multiple times. Granted, those boys are close to useless, but even when the knights show up, these guys are beating them now.

And the knights aren't bad. The knights are scary. 20' tall suits, like giant killer robots from some low budget flick, rolling and cutting and dodging, throwing plasma from their swords, rockets, all that—and they're getting beat. I mean, these boys got armor like a space cruiser and they know all the tricks. Decent mercs with top of the line stuff shouldn't be able to take them out. Even a squad of Wardogs would have some serious trouble on their hands if one of these knights came a-knocking."

Pitt's report was cut short when the pair of contract guys showed up with a rolling cart overflowing with food. Fruit, sandwiches, hot coffee, soydeens, pastries, *Ocean Octaves*, hard candy, all sorts of good stuff.

"Not bad at all," Squid said, taking a pastry and a cup of black coffee. "If this is you just throwing together some snacks, my hat's off."

"We do what we can," Pitt said, tearing open a bag of chips. "They stuck me in logistics for a reason."

"Wish we'd had you on a few dozen other missions I could rattle off," Squid said. "So, these mysterious mercenaries are good, then. No leads on the outfit? SecSec, maybe? Thompson's?"

"Nope," Pitt said. "None of the regulars. Or irregulars, for that matter. You ask me, I'd say they were from out there somewhere." He waved his hand towards the scarlet sky. "Way out there."

"Aliens?" Ward said.

"It's as good a guess as any," Pitt said. "Whispers are all over, you know. Darned if I know what they want here or what they're getting paid, but they're giving Axios an edge it's never had before, and the Sfodrian military is shook like soda pop in a dropship."

Lord General Landros was a hulking man with a vented metal neck brace and a puckered white scar across most of the left side of his face, directly across the eye socket. The eye on that side was a blank silver sphere that looked more like a full-spectrum sensor rather than a conventional syntheye. His upper lip was notched into a sneer where the scar crossed it—and his attitude pretty well matched the expression on his face.

"So you're it?" he asked as he looked us over. We'd changed into our armor, all polished and impersonal. Our mirrored visors made identification impossible. Only Yost wasn't suited up.

"Yes, this is it," Captain Yost said. "The best money can buy. Did you want us to send for more men? I can certainly have our sales liaison draw up a contract." The captain had been sent ahead of us by two weeks. He'd commanded Red Skull company for a decade before becoming what you might call a circuit captain, working a variety front-line gigs outside the Ascendancy to "get some fresh air," as he told us before our meeting. Yost had a good reputation, although in my opinion no one was up to Marks's caliber.

"We prefer to invest in our own men," Landros said, his sneer becoming more pronounced. "Sfodria has a reputation to keep up."

"Of course," Yost said. "Your knights are most impressive."

" 'Unlike the militia,' I expect you are thinking."

"I said nothing of the sort," Yost replied.

"And yet it is true," the Lord General said, thumping his fist on the steel wall of the chamber. There were no chairs in this conference room, which I assumed was some sort of local custom. No items of comfort at all, in fact. Not even carpeting. The floor was a tessellation of red and black tiles and there were some stylized tapestries of battle scenes hanging on the wall, but no furniture. "The militia is of the common people, and the common people are not the nation."

Yost waited silently as the Lord General thumped the wall again for emphasis. "Our knights are the nation. And they are failing, which has led us to realize the weakness of our position. We have plenty of manpower upon which we can draw, but that manpower is common, undertrained, and poorly equipped." He looked us over again, moving up to Park and tapping on his visor with his knuckles. Park didn't move and the Lord General grunted his approval. "Your man doesn't even flinch. I have asked in the past for a proper force of men, men who will kill and die without fear, but the knights have borne everything on their shoulders."

"We are willing to train your men to be what you request," Yost said mildly.

"As much as it pains me, it seems our polity needs the commoners to play a more active role. My family has agreed, as have the knights."

"You are of the Oukiton bloodline," Yost said. "I have read your history. It is an impressive military tradition."

The Lord General gave him a look that appeared almost approving. "You did your research. I myself would still be a knight if it were not for certain medical impediments. Unfortunately, our traditional methods of war have been crafted for the knighthood, not for commoners. Hence our need for commoners to teach them."

Captain Yost smiled slightly. "We'll shape them up. Has the government approved a budget?"

"Yes," Landros said, producing a circular tablet from an interior pocket of his slate-gray uniform. "Look at these numbers."

Yost took the tablet and scanned through. He raised an eyebrow. "This is three times the budget we discussed, Lord General."

The Lord General nodded. "It has become apparent to the Stratocracy that the problem has become more urgent in recent weeks. We will also add a ten percent bonus to the agreed-upon contract. I will expect you to begin your review tomorrow. You are dismissed."

Yost nodded, looking thoughtful. He knew, as we all did, that this was not going to be a cakewalk. Only a truly desperate client would ever TRIPLE his budget.

The motel smelled like boiled cabbage but it was cleaner than a lot of places we've bivouacked in the past. We tried to order meals but the kitchen staff shook their heads. "We don't do made-to-order meals," explained a young man as the older guy in the kitchen muttered and cursed to himself. "We only serve communal meals here."

"Communal?" Jock said. "You guys some sort of utopian nutcases? I require a special diet for medical reasons. Write this down, bud: I want a half a roasted chicken and a bottle of red wine, even if you need to go rob a farm."

"Cool it," Squid said, taking Jock's arm. "When in Rhysalan, as they say."

"We're not in Rhysalan," Jock said.

"Enough," Squid said, then turned to the kitchen guy. "Listen, kid. Feed us whatever's back there and I'll try to make sure the boys don't beat you to death."

The guy swallowed hard and went back to the kitchen, then came out again shortly with metal bowls filled with some sort of gruel.

"Oh, hell no," Jones said, sniffing the stuff. "This smells like catfish vomit."

"It's a fish-and-grain porridge," Yost said, speaking for the first time since the meeting with the Lord General. "I've been eating it for weeks. Nutritious."

"We have plenty of funds now," Ward said around a mouthful of gruel. "Can't we see about maybe having at least an autochef sent over and stocked. Or maybe some decent MREs? We get some of those with our stuff, Squid?"

"We did," Squid replied, "but they're for missions, not for our stay here."

"Quit bitching," Park said, shoving a spoonful of porridge into his mouth. "It's good."

"That settles it," Jones said. "It's officially inedible."

"Enough about the food," Zelag said. "We got a lot more money to work with now. Captain, weren't we supposed to be just advising? This looks like a serious revamp to our core objectives."

"Yes," Yost said, taking a bowl of soup and sitting down. "We'll start our in-depth review tomorrow and see where we need to go from here."

"Get 'em some better armor," Ward said. "And at least some PN-60s. They're still on the 40 platform according to what I looked up."

"Hardware isn't the answer," Jones argued. "Training, training, training. Give 'em better rifles and we could still take out these militia jokers using pointed sticks. Lord General doesn't give a rat's ass about the commoners, as he calls them, and it shows."

"No pride," Ward said. "No reason to fight."

"I don't know," Zelag said. "I think it's hard to reach any conclusions when we haven't even talked with the men yet. We need to get a feel for the culture before we try to make any drastic changes."

"Drastic changes are just what they need, Zee!" Jock spoke up from the end of the table. "We got a real budget now. Jones is right about the training, but let's get a helluva a lot of good, useful stuff for them to train on. Get them up to date and turn them into a proper fighting force in one swoop. Right, Tommy?"

"I don't know," I said. "Without a solid sitrep, I'm not feeling it." I stopped and pinched some chunky salt crystals out of a bowl and sprinkled them on my cooling gruel, giving myself a chance to think. "Intel first, then analysis. For now, let's just stick to the plan."

"Yeah," Zelag said. "Tommy gets it."

"They need heavy gun platforms," Ace yelled.

"And chemical weapons," Park added.

"And an orbital death station, by God!" Jones added vehemently, slamming down his fist and upending his gruel.

"You bastards really are the bloodthirstiest sons of bitches I've ever met," Squid said, lighting a cigar. "I'm getting a little misty over here."

Captain Yost scraped a final spoonful out of his bowl and ate it, then put the spoon down and looked around. "Well, now that you all got that out of your system, most of you will be glad to know that I have indeed decided to revise the plan."

There were some cheers from the table. Zelag looked at me and shrugged. Hey, we tried.

"We'll have Pitt look into weapons and armor, starting tomorrow. I'll work out a budget with accounting and see where we'll go from here. In the meantime, Falkland, you're going to go out with Ward, Zelag and Jones and do a little recon. Squid tells me you four have worked together before. You say we need intel, so go get some. Get out in the field, look at some of the previous engagements, and link in with the militia." The captain got up to leave. "I'll expect a full report within a week."

"Dammit, Tommy," Zelag said once the captain was gone. "You went and got us homework."

"Hey, you were on my side," I shot back, feeling betrayed.

"You're part of the problem too, Zelag," Jones said. "You and Tommy have been straight-up downers this time out."

"In fairness, they may have kept us from dying in space," Ward pointed out. "Or being sold into slavery by pirates."

"Maybe," Jones said. "Of course, for all we know, the *Gondola* was hijacked by bikini models looking for handsome sex slaves. Still, Tommy, you should've shut your big mouth this time."

"Yeah, you're probably right," I said. "Trust me, I'm not thrilled either."

Trying to figure out what would help these amateurs was a job for analysts. I'd rather just worry about me and my team. I wasn't an analyst, I wasn't an officer, and I wasn't logistics like Pitt. Or even a specialist nerd like Edgerton.

But that didn't matter now. For the next week, we were Wardogs Force Recon, whether we liked it or not.

Chapter 5

The Sfodrian militia were the crummiest group of soldiers I've ever seen. I mean, they were even worse than those actors who do historical reenactments with bags of fake blood hidden in their uniforms, timed to burst when they get shot by lasers built into their antique retro-guns. Seriously, those reenactors are observably better than the Sfodrians. At least they can follow orders and stand in a straight line.

I spent the day after we arrived reviewing everything I could find on the militia. Most of it was data already collected by Pitt and Yost with help from Jimbo the AI. I ignored the considerably more massive amount of information available on the knights, since they weren't relevant to my assignment. What I found was that the militia was called up according to long-standing families and land contracts that allegedly dated back to the landing of the original colonists. It didn't matter if a militia member was a doctor or worked as a cleaning bot maintenance tech, if his family was on the commoner list and he was of the proper age, he had to go when called, and there was no pay in it for him. It was a duty to the state. I had to admit, that I'd say to hell with the state if I was in the same situation.

I decided to strike out beyond the initial reports and jack in to the local net. After ten minutes of near-fruitless poking around, I realized that the subject must be heavily censored by the Sfodrian government. National security, no doubt. I got up from the little desk in my room and stretched. I'd been sitting too long. Ward looked up from the book he was reading. "So, Tommy. You got it all worked out now?"

"There isn't much to work with," I said. "Net seems to be censored so all I've got is what Yost and Pitt already threw together with that old AI box. I got enough to learn that the system is a mess, though. Guys don't even get paid. They're basically hereditary cannon fodder. You can't expect to teach them any discipline, morale, or esprit de corps when they're actually incentivized to desert!"

"Maybe try to give them a sense of purpose," Ward said with a shrug. "My son sometimes spends an hour or two filling up a cup with pebbles, then dumping them out, then filling it up again. He seems to find fulfillment in that."

"Sure, and if the Sfodrians were drafting three-year-olds, I'd say you're onto something. There's no point in even trying to think about this until we go out with them on a mission, see what's cooking."

"Sounds like a party," Ward said absently. He'd already tuned out and was back reading his book.

"I'll just go talk to the captain about jumping in, then," I said. He ignored me, so I walked out to look for Captain Yost. Me and my big, stupid mouth.

"Welcome, sirs," a redheaded guy in a saggy brown uniform with a round, bronzed face greeted us, saluting with a thumped fist on the chest. I couldn't tell what his rank was but I mirrored the salute, as did Zelag. Ward and Jones half-waved, which was about as diplomatic as they ever got. Pitt made some arrangements and a driver took us over to the nearby Sfodrian militia base. We put on our battlesuits but left the helmets off, opting for hats and shades instead. I figured it would humanize us a bit, maybe let us connect better. I also lathered up with all-weather sunscreen, as did the other guys. It was sunny and hot outside and I'd rather avoid the radiation.

"I'm the citizen in charge of today's mission," the guy said. "I am Stylen Gardoros."

"What's your rank?" I asked.

"I am a commoner," he replied, as if that explained anything. "Though I have been appointed Overseer for the current call-up."

"Great," I said. "I'm Corporal Falkland with Wardogs Incorporated. This is Zelag, Jones and Ward."

"What did you hope to do today, sirs?" Gardoros asked. "We don't have much time to talk, as our two decades have a mission we've been ordered to undertake in a few short minutes."

"I know. We're going with you," I said.

"Decades?" Jones said, looking puzzled.

"Units of ten," Gardoros said, waving around at a group of uniformed men slouching around five battered Toymo jeeps. "Doesn't your force have any organization?"

I heard Ward suppress a snort.

"It's a different organizational system," I said. "What you call a decade, we would call a squad."

He nodded. "All right. Well, who ordered you to accompany us?"

"One of the knights. Sir Something-or-other. I can't even pronounce his name."

As I expected, Gardoros wasn't about to question anything that even might have come down from on high. He nodded.

"Certainly, sirs. It would be our honor to go to war with famous warriors such as yourselves!"

The other militia guys looked warily at us as we walked over. In our armor, we dwarfed even the biggest of them.

"You guys are mercenaries. You actually kill people for money?" one of them asked. He was a middle-aged guy, a little overweight with thick hands like a laborer.

"Damn straight," Jones said. "No payee, no killee. What about you?"

"We fight for the Lords," the man said, standing straighter. "As did our fathers before us."

"Good for you," Jones said, rolling his eyes.

"We're hoping to help you learn how to fight a little more effectively," Zelag said, trying to smooth things over. "Get you better set up and organized."

"We know how to fight," another guy chimed in. This guy looked like a banking clerk. He was thin, with pencil-like arms and a prominent Adam's apple.

"Sure," Jones said. "That's why the Axiosi keep kicking your asses."

The guy stood up a little straighter, eyes flashing, and I half-expected him to put up his fists. Well, at least he had some fight in him.

"Don't worry," Jones said, relenting a little and clapping the guy on the shoulder. "The Lord General and our captain have got some good ideas for you. We'll get you fixed up. Honest, we ain't the enemy."

"In truth, we could use some assistance," Gardoros admitted. "We've never heard of our knights losing before. If they can't defeat the Axi, what chance to do we have?"

"We'll fight to the death," the guy with thick hands said bravely, if unconvincingly.

"Let's try to keep you all alive first," I said. "So tell me, Gardoros, what's the mission?"

"We have an info gathering patrol to the location of a grave crime. As you no doubt know, two of our noble knights were lost this week. We have determined the area to be clear of enemy at this point and our job is to determine what happened to them. There's also an Axiosi patrol that was spotted this morning a bit farther out—we'll see if we can find them and take them out, if possible."

"Very good," I said. "Lead on. We'll observe and render what assistance we can."

A few minutes later we loaded up the jeeps, only to find one of the five wouldn't start. After some arguing back and forth with the base mechanic and a failed attempt to jump start it, we were packed into four jeeps. We locked our helmets on just in case the Sfodrians were as bad at driving as they were at vehicle maintenance. The heat of the sun was already getting to us and our battlesuits are much better at temperature regulation with their helmets on.

It's also easier to talk amongst ourselves, and we did.

"These guys are hopeless," Jones said over his com so the Sfodrians couldn't hear.

"No officers," Zelag said.

"No training," Ward added.

"No chili," Jones said.

"Yeah, but they're the client," I said. "Don't be total jackasses if you can help it."

"The government is the client," Jones said. "Or the knights. Though I guess they are the government. These guys are total POGs."

"Yeah, I know," I admitted. "They have no clue. But they're really just draftees, after all. What more can you expect of them?"

We hit a bump and I grabbed onto the handle. The four of us were jammed into the back seat of the jeep and it felt like whatever shocks the thing may have had were long-lost somewhere in the dust of this godforsaken planet.

"Look," Ward said, pointing up at the gun mounted on top of the Toymo. "There's a PN-60 for you."

"Space," Jones said. "So it is. They mounted a freaking PN-60 as their vehicle gun. That's gotta be the most ridiculous thing I've ever seen."

I shook my head at the dust-covered rifle. They were good guns, but you'd figure they'd go for at least the long-range 120 or even a good old-fashioned rapid fire projectile gun. Nope. It was a standard issue PN-60.

Zelag patted his blue rifle. "Maybe we can borrow it if these Feem-pers give out on us."

"Let's hope not," Ward said. "That thing looks like it's long overdue for a good cleaning. Contacts and the plasma chamber are probably corroded to hell."

We hit another bump and it felt like the seat beneath me gave a little too much. I thumped myself up and down a couple of times to see. Yeah, it was loose.

"We're just gonna park in a minute and walk to where the incident took place," our driver yelled back to us. "Terrain is too rough to drive, and maybe we can take them by surprise if we come in on foot."

I looked back at the huge trail of dust following in our wake and laughed in disbelief. Surprise. Yeah, that seemed likely.

We parked the vehicles and walked about a kilometer up the side of a cactus-covered ridge. At the top, we looked down into a valley where a dry stream bed lay amidst huge boulders and the ruined columns of an ancient temple.

"There was a report of some enemy activity in this area," Gardoros told us as we walked down the hillside. "Since the militia was in the middle of a base rotation, Sir Hexarvald and Sir Joshimo traveled together. A drone went first and spotted a small force before going blank. The enemy force should have been easy for two knights to handle. Yet even as their families watched the live feed of their exploits, they were cut down in an ambush."

"Do you have those recordings?" I asked him.

"Oh no," he said, looking appalled. "They belong to their families. Such dishonor can never be viewed by commoners!"

"Oh, for–" Jones expostulated over the com.

"Shut up, Jonesy!" I cut him off and turned off my external speaker.

"They entered the valley there, and there," Gardoros said, pointing. "You can still see the impressions of their mighty strides."

There were two sets of deep indentations entering the valley from the east, that ended on the other side of the stream bed where the ground was scorched and broken.

"That must be where they rolled in," Jones said even as I made the observation.

"I was told they were hit on several sides at once," Gardoros said.

"Don't they have pretty good armor?" Ward asked.

"Mighty armor," Gardoros replied. "The Axiosi soldiers have never carried weapons heavy enough to harm a knight. Two knights together should have been indestructible."

"Looks like they were taken out pretty damn fast," Ward noted as we reached the spot of the ambush and saw scorch marks and turned earth. "If they were tearing it up and fighting back like that other guy we saw, they would have left a lot more damage to the ground."

"Geez, how big are their suits?" Zelag said over the com as he looked into a large rut. "This is a little damage? The ground looks pretty damn ripped up to me."

I looked around to see where the knights might have been hit from. A few large boulders looked like good locations to hide, plus the fallen remains of a temple wall were at a good height for hiding behind and shooting over.

One of the Sfodrian militia members was taking pictures of the entire area. A few of the soldiers gathered in a group by the stream bed and took off their hats and put them over their chests for a group shot.

"What are they doing?" I asked. "Why take group photos here?"

"They are showing their respect for the fallen knights. They will offer the image as a tribute to them at the memorial."

"I wonder if the Axiosi are hiring," Jones muttered. Ward laughed bitterly.

Gardoros stopped for a moment and put his hand to his ear. "Yes, Overseer. Thank you."

He turned to me. "The enemy patrol has been located and our decades have been honored with the duty to engage it. Do you wish to join us in battle?"

"It is our fondest wish," I said, ignoring the sarcastic comments in my ear. "Let's see what our Axiosi friends have got!"

Since the patrol was on foot, we closed in on them in under a local hour. The AI in our buckets scanned them in once we were close enough, revealing an eight-man squad ahead.

"Stop here," Gardoros ordered the drivers and they came to a halt behind a group of boulders and cacti. "We'll move in on them on foot," he announced. "Let's head in."

The guys jumped out and started moving towards the enemy's position, using boulders as cover.

"Screw this," Ward said over our coms. "We can get a jump on them by cutting down and around. Let them face off with the Sfodrians and we'll get behind the targets."

"Sounds like a plan," I said, and the four of us took off at a right angle down into the brush of a trickling stream bed. I saw Gardoros looking down at us in confusion and saluted him, then we disappeared into cover.

"Those guys have no tactics," Jones said. "I could take all of them out myself."

"Too bad they're our clients," Zelag said. "I'd help."

"Enough of that," I said. "Like I said, they're civvies."

"POGs," Ward said.

"Fine, POGs—but they're our guys for now." I glanced at the enemy position and saw they were balled up behind some rocks. I wondered if they had any heavier artillery with them—and as I had the thought, I heard the *THUMP* of an RPG or some other incendiary and watched the dots of the friendlies scattering about.

The enemy targets were almost to our right now and I hoped they didn't have the same scanning tech we had. They were sitting tight behind cover as we passed.

"I could use some better topographical data," Ward said.

"Agreed," I said. "We should have tried for access to satellite before coming out."

"Eyes and scanners will be fine," Jones said. "These guys are stone age."

We moved around behind the enemy and looked for a good ambush point.

"Tommy, you think we can hit them with the wide EMP?" Zelag asked.

"We don't know if their armor is digital," I replied. "Or if their guns will toast when the pulse hits."

"Just watch out for my arm," Zelag reminded us.

"We can move up the bank here," Ward said, pointing up the rocky embankment. "That big boulder is decent cover and will get us close enough for plasma."

"Let's do it," I said, and we booked it up the bank and got behind the boulder. Then I saw enemy movement on our direction—a team of four.

"They must have scanners too," Jones said.

"Stay behind cover," I said.

"They're moving around—splitting up," Zelag said, but I'd already noted the movement in my display.

"Alright, Ward—hit them with the EMP first," I said. "Widest angle. Zelag, get behind him just in case."

Ward moved up a crack in the boulder and sighted up, then fired with plasma off. There was a zapping sound but no light—it wasn't something you could see. One of the two guys approaching fell down twitching but the other kept coming.

"One down," Ward said. "Dispersion should have hit both."

"Probably implants in that guy," Zelag muttered. "I'm beginning to rethink my prosthetic options at this point."

"Take it off and we'll find you a nice meathook or something," Jones told him sympathetically.

We moved into good firing positions around the edges of the boulder, then opened up with plasma on the second guy and took him down.

At that point, the Sfodrians were engaged in an active firefight with two other Axiosi teams. Their marksmanship was such that neither party appeared to be in much danger of actually hitting the other.

CRACK! There was a massive explosion, throwing rock and dust around us. Ward came rolling down off the top of the boulder almost on my head.

"RPG!" Zelag yelled.

"You think? Take them out!" I yelled, seeing last two enemy dots abandon their cover and move off on a tear towards a nearby ridge. My heart caught in my throat as I looked down at Ward laying on the ground. His suit was coated with dust and debris, but he pulled himself into a sitting position.

"I'm fine, Tommy," he said over the com. "Dropped my damn gun on the other side though."

"Got one!" Jones announced.

"And the other is down," Zelag reported as he lowered his rifle.

I breathed a sigh of relief and watched as half the Sfodrians charged the enemy position after hurling about ten grenades that didn't land anywhere near the four Axiosi keeping their heads down behind the rocks. Not that what passed for the suppressive fire being laid down by the other Sfodrian decade was likely to hit them.

One enterprising Axiosi popped up long enough to take out two charging Sfodrians before I heard a familiar *fiss-crack* to my left and the guy's head vanished in a bright plume of plasma, blood, and brains.

"You nail him, Cyborg?" I asked Zelag.

"One shot, one kill."

"You've still got it," I said.

"RPG hit about two meters down from my feet" Ward said. "Not going to get me that easily."

"It's just as well," Jones said. "I forgot to bring a camera for the memorial shot anyhow."

We moved around the boulder to rejoin the militia. Ward picked up his rifle and whistled, holding it up. The barrel was bent at a 45-degree angle to one side, with a chunk missing at the bend.

"Well, you never liked it anyway," Zelag said. "Maybe we can borrow that PN-60 for you."

"Good thing that wasn't my head," Ward said as we moved towards the Sfodrians, who were finishing their enthusiastic attempt to emulate a hog butcher with a personal vendetta against all things porcine.

"You wouldn't miss it," Jones said. "Probably costs less than that rifle."

Gardoros turned and waved a bloody hand as we approached. "We successfully overran the position, Wardogs," he announced. "The battle is won!"

"Good work," I said.

"Your assistance was most welcome," he thanked us. "Your diversion was clever. You kept them distracted for us."

"Glad to hear it," I said, and refrained from pointing out that we'd accounted for five-eighths of the enemy dead, or that they had somehow managed to take three casualties despite a five-to-one numerical advantage in their favor. A win is a win, after all.

"We should grab their weapons for analysis," Ward said.

"You just want a new rifle," Jones said.

"No, he's right," I said. "We need to know how these guys are taking out their knights."

We hunted around and picked up a few plasma rifles and an empty RPG. I didn't recognize the make on either. The Axiosi had helmets with displays inside, so I grabbed one that looked intact and we headed back to the jeeps.

"You know," Zelag said as we rode back to base. "We'd probably get a lot more intel on these guys if we captured a couple of them alive."

"An officer, in particular," Ward said.

"Yeah," Jones said, warming to the topic. "That would be fun. I'd love to have a little chat with a few of them."

I winced thinking about the mess that Jones's chats tended to leave behind, but I had to agree with him. Catch an officer, they'd give us a lot more info on whoever these guys were working with. More info was what we desperately needed if we were going to solve this situation.

"What have we learned already?" I asked the guys, hoping we could work over some of the day's experiences and maybe synthesize some ideas.

"That the Sfodrian militia can't shoot straight," Jones said.

"Yes, and?" I asked.

"The other guys can't either."

"But the knights got taken down fast," Ward said.

"Right," I agreed. "How?"

"Surprise," Jones said.

"Yeah, but these guys we just took out were amateur hour," Zelag said. "How would they take a couple of guys in sophisticated robotic battlesuits out?"

"Jammers," Ward said. "They knocked down a drone before the ambush, right?"

"Yeah," I agreed. "They could at least do that. But a little camera drone is child's play. Apparently the knights have suits more sophisticated than ours—and they weren't jamming us at all."

"Their mercenary friends must have done it," Zelag said. "We already know they have serious cloaking."

"Yeah," I said. "They must have jammed them, so the knights rolled into their position blind, then were taken out somehow."

"Probably not with these rifles," Zelag said, gesturing to the pile of weapons rattling about on the floorboard. "These are Popov knock-offs."

"Really?" Ward said. "They don't look like PNs to me."

"Trust the gun collector," Zelag said, picking one of them up. "These are modded. Notice the barrel—similar to our normal carry. Older model, though. PN-50. It's just the stock that's been changed out. It's a solid composite instead of being screwed together like the regular model."

"Whaddya know," Jones said, looking at the rifle. "It is! I see the manufacturer's stamp, then another one underneath."

"Probably a special contract," Ward said. "I read SportCo Re-mod. PN-50, too. I think I will take one for myself."

"Maybe you can mount it on an ancient Toymo," Jones said.

"Maybe I will."

I laughed, then called in to HQ, gave Yost and Squid the sitrep, and explained our intention to grab an officer for interrogation.

"Good idea," Yost replied. "But not you guys. Come back to base and write up the AAR. We'll send out another team."

It seemed like a good plan at the time. But then, everyone's got a plan, right up until the moment they get shot in the face.

Chapter 6

By the time we got back to base, I found out Jock, Park, Cole and Ace had already taken off to join two platoons of Sfodrian militia in a hunt for an Axiosi officer of our very own. Yost didn't play around. "Falkland," he said as I walked into the cafeteria area looking for coffee. The other guys had headed to the showers but I needed to clear my head a bit. I could have just taking a stimulant hit from my suit, but technically I wasn't in combat at the moment and a hit would be a 20-credit deduction from the week's pay. "I'm going to have Morrel and Edgerton help you hunt down some officer material for the militia."

"Me?" I said. "Why me?"

"Because you know more about them than anyone," Yost shrugged. "Morrel has a background in personnel and Edgerton's got an AI to help you sort faster. Plus, he's smart. I've gotten you permission to access the Sfodrian military computer archives, though you'll have to do it through a console they provided." He sighed. "These people and their secrets. I already gave the console to Edgerton but it's coded to your retina so he says he can't do anything with it."

"I'm on it, sir," I said.

"Good," he said. "What's this I hear about Ward already losing his Feemper?"

"RPG near-miss took it out. Not his fault, sir."

"Dammit! Those things are not cheap! Well, that's why we brought a few spares."

"Good thing, sir."

"Well, get on with it, Falkland. And try not to lose your damn rifle!"

"Yes, sir!"

The shower lacked a hot setting. I've been a lot of weird places, but a world with this tech level that lacked hot water was a new one. The cold water at least woke me up a bit, as did the chocolate bar I liberated from Ward's pack. There was a knock at the door. I threw on a shirt and opened it to find Morrel and Edgerton outside. The latter held the locked console.

"Come in," I said, waving them in. "You want to work with me at the desk here or find someplace else?"

"Here is fine with me," Morrel said. He was a short, dark-haired guy with a single eyebrow. Edgerton handed me the console and I set it on the desk and powered it up, then sat in front of the screen and let it scan my retina. It made a few grinding noises, then unlocked. "Can your AI work with it when it's open?" I asked Edgerton.

"We'll see," he said, pulling up one of the two hard plastic chairs that came with the room. He blinked a few times, then the screen on the console went black. "Nope."

"Great," I said, cursing the paranoid Sfodrians. I let it scan my retina again and it opened. "You'll just have to look over my shoulder, I guess. Maybe your AI can help somehow."

"It won't be any faster, Falkland," he said. "I'll look, though."

"We should have authorized him as well," Morrel said.

"That would be abso-freaking-lutely great," I said. "Who would we talk to?"

"Pitt would probably know," Morrel said. "I think he's down at the hangar.

I shook my head. This was going to be a pain in the neck.

Two hours later, the computer was unlocked by somebody in the government, authorizing both Edgerton and Morrel to help out temporarily. We were informed that the permission was only granted for eight hours and would need a manual reset after we submitted another request.

I decided to try and not take that long, though when I saw the 100,000-plus individual profiles, my heart sank. "This is going to take forever," I said. "I don't think there are even this many people in the militia."

"No," Morrel said. "It's less than half that. Some of these are probably dead or not active."

"It's okay," Edgerton said. "Babbage can sort it for us."

"Have at it," I said. "Here's what I want to see: I want guys that have long-term experience, with good records and no serious marks against them."

Edgerton and his AI started flying through records faster than I could read. A few minutes passed, then he said, "Down to 16,436 now."

"How about weapons certs?" Morrel said. "Experience across multiple platforms would be good. Maybe flight ability plus armored experience as well?"

"Throw some of that in there," I said to Edgerton.

He kept scanning. "3,476 with moderate to high levels of experience serving in different areas."

"Is there any intelligence test info?" Morrel asked.

"You think that's important?" I asked. "I've served under some officers without much going on upstairs."

"And how did that work out?"

"Not great," I admitted. "Not generally. All right, fair enough. Sarge, can you sort by intelligence?"

"Yeah, I think so. Babbage is working on it." He ran his fingers through his hair with one hand while he swished through records with the other. "Yep, okay. We have more background data from their civilian records. Schools here do test for intelligence."

"Get rid of the top 15% and the bottom 75%," Morrel said.

"Really?" Edgerton replied. "You don't want the smartest?"

"Yeah," I agreed. "Don't we want the best guys?"

"No way," Morrel said. "The smartest guys don't make the best leaders. You want smart, but not too smart. The rocket scientists won't listen to anyone or follow orders well. They also can't communicate effectively with the men."

"Makes sense when you put it that way," I nodded, and silently pointed at Edgerton behind his back. Morrel laughed.

"All right," Edgerton said, clueless. "So now we're down to 521."

"At this point, I guess we could just go through them one by one," Morrel said. "See if anything pops out to us. Or maybe look for the best records, service awards. I don't know, Tommy. What do you think?"

I thought for a moment of other things I'd like to see in an officer. Respect, courage under fire, decisiveness, and self-confidence. And, ideally, stone cold ruthlessness where protecting their men was concerned. They were things that were hard to quantify, but we needed info. Then I had a thought.

"Can we pull up all their faces, just their faces, and see what they look like?"

"That's a weird way to pick an officer," Edgerton said. "Doesn't make any logical sense."

"Yeah," I admitted. "Maybe. But I'm thinking, there's sometimes just this look you can see."

"Sure," Morrel said. "I know what you're talking about. But I don't know if you can see it in a picture."

"Tommy!" Ward said, crashing through the door without an introduction. "We got trouble. Suit up—we need to move, now!"

"Our squad that went out with the militia got themselves pinned down," Yost told us, throwing me the keys to a Sfodrian jeep. "Two RPGs are already in the back. Take your team and break them out. I'm also putting you in charge of Privates Jordan, Kopenni, Roq and Ford." I saw the other guys putting on their helmets and nodded at them. "Four knights will be joining up with you momentarily. Also, all of you, scan this. It's Sfodrian GPS access."

He pulled out a small data chip and handed it to me. "It's been sketchy but it may be of some help."

"Yes sir," I replied, scanning the chip and watching as my helmet overlaid the new information on my screen. "We got the knights' com channel?" I asked.

"Negative on that," he replied, to my surprise. "Just don't let them step on you."

"Step on us?" Jones said to me as we got in our jeep.

"They're pretty damn big," I said. "We'll take point," I told Ford as he started the second jeep. I handed Jones the chip and pushed the starter on our Toymo. To my surprise, it started smoothly enough. Ward and Zelag climbed in the back and Jones passed the chip to them as I took off onto the dirt road leading in the direction of our unit showing on my visor.

"I hope these knights fight better than the militia," Ward said.

"Expensive doesn't mean these guys are great, though," Jones said. "I've seen some expensive vehicles wrapped around bridge columns."

"Truth," Ward said.

We were only a few kilos away from the action when the ground started to shake and a roaring noise filled the air. At first I thought the jeep was breaking apart, then I realized something was approaching fast from behind.

"We've got airborne bogeys coming in behind us," Ford said over the com.

"DUDE!" Ward yelled. "Will you look at that?"

"I'm driving!" I yelled back. "What is it?"

"It's our escort!" Zelag laughed. "It's the knights! They're gigantic flying robots!"

As he said it, four gigantic figures like massive statues rocketed over our heads and I saw what the guys had seen. Imagine a 20-foot tall robotic man spouting gouts of rocket fire and flying like a metallic vulture over your head at near Mach 1 and you'll get the idea of what I was feeling. It was crazy. I couldn't help but gawk. I've seen a lot of ships and weapons and all that, but these guys were something else.

"I want a suit like that," Jones announced. "In red. With giant glowing plasma horns."

"Better save up for one," Ward said. "I don't think they give them to commoners like you."

"We're closing in on our guys," Zelag said. "From the satellite images, it looks like they're inside a ring of ruins. Looks like two infantry platoons have them pinned, but they've got armored units closing in from east and south."

I switched my com channel to see if I could raise Jock. "Scotsman, we're on our way. You holding out?"

"Roger that, Fox," came the reply amidst the crackle of plasma and the sound of yells and explosions. "We're holding our own at the moment, but we got minitanks incoming. Maybe one or two-man jobs. We tried hitting them at extreme range with the Feempers but they seem to be unaffected."

"Roger," I said. "Sit tight. We're bringing in the cavalry."

"Cavalry?" he replied, then I heard some more plasma fire. "Oh, you got some knights with you?"

"Roger on that," I replied. "Four are airborne and just flew over the ridge in front of us. You should see them any moment now."

"The ridge…there! I see 'em!" he yelled. "Holy hell, look at those monsters!"

"Be there in a few," I said. "Over."

We stopped at the ridge and abandoned our jeeps. I assigned Jordan and Zelag the RPGs and we clambered over the ridge on foot. We looked down into the valley in time to see two Sfodrian knights facing off against three squadrons of minitanks as Axiosi infantry scattered to find cover. My display showed the other two knights hovering over the other side of the circle of ruins where the Sfodrian militia and Wardogs were pinned down, sending huge blasts of fire from their swords down into the enemy ranks.

"We've got more enemy incoming!" Jones said. "Look to the west. Off behind us a bit, there!"

I zoomed out my tactical view but my sensors hadn't picked them up yet. But I was able to see a column of dust rising from beyond a patch of twisted trees.

"The knights have it under control down there," I said. I saw a minitank exploded as one of the knights sent a rocket through its armor. "Let's see if we can get eyes on the incoming."

We moved along the ridge and into the woods. They were a lot thinner when you got close. The ground was mostly cracked earth and gravel around scattered trees.

"RPGs, lock and load," I ordered. "Everyone take cover. If this is a column of tanks, just stay down. Don't engage, we'll just call it in to the big boys below."

Ward and I took cover inside a patch of twisted trees with 10-centimeter thorns. Thank Ares for armor, I thought, as I pressed myself against a trunk that would have torn me up if I were in civvies.

My heart thumped and my palms sweated as my helmet mic picked up the sounds of engines as well as feet marching. There were definitely vehicles incoming. I checked my display and saw the heat signatures of two of minitanks and a half-dozen enemy infantry blink into view. Then another four minitanks appeared on screen, as well as another dozen men.

"We can take 'em," Ward said.

"You sure about that?" I said. "We don't know their armor or what sort of penetration they'll take."

"These are light one-man jobs," Jordan said. "Tin cans."

"And we have Feempers," Jones added. "We jam up the first few, pick off the soldiers, maybe stop the advance."

"You heard Jock. The Feempers didn't work. Maybe they went old school."

"At extreme range," Jones said. "We're going to hit them nice and close."

I shouldered my rifle and looked through the scope. I could feel the climate control in my helmet compensating for the cold sweat on my forehead. I didn't see the approaching column yet, but my visor told me it was close.

I thought it through. We could hit them as they passed, find out our weapons were ineffectual, and risk getting torn to shreds. Or, if the Feempers and RPGs were capable, we'd take them out quickly. Or we could let them pass, then harry them from behind, putting them between us and the knights. I looked ahead towards a point where the rocks made a natural bottleneck. They'll roll through there, I thought. If we can take out the point vehicle, we can trap them there..

"Retreat beyond that bottleneck," I ordered. "We'll hit them with everything we've got as the first vehicle comes through those rocks. If it's not immobilized, we run like hell, got it? Now move!"

We ran through the brush and got to the other side of the bottleneck and broke up into four two-man teams. I was with Ward

"They're coming," I said, seeing the movement of the tanks and men on my visor. "Steady. When the first two tanks are between the rocks, let them have it."

I raised my rifle to my shoulder and watched the gap. Four infantry came through, moving forwards. They looked around, then I saw them raise their rifles expectantly.

"They're seeing us," Ward hissed.

They must have picked us up on their scanners—but as they scanned, I spotted the tanks still rolling in towards the gap behind them. Stupid—first thing I would have done was stop the column if I was seeing enemy beyond a chokepoint. They must have thought we were simply crummy Sfodrian militia troops and not any kind of threat.

"Ready," I said. "Watch for them to move in."

Then three things happened almost at once. First, lead elements of the enemy infantry opened fire towards where they believed we were based on their scanners. Second, the first minitank emerged from the gap. And third, I yelled "FIRE!" just as it came out, and the two grenades were away, along with six high-intensity blasts of combined electro-magnetic pulse and plasma.

I couldn't tell how many direct hits we got on the first tank, as there was a big explosion of dirt and rocks as at least one of the grenades hit a rock instead of the tank, hurling a small plume of rubble, dust, and smoke skyward. Our fire had exposed our positions to the infantry. I switched my Feemper to broad dispersion and fired it in case any of them had implants. No effect—but it didn't matter anyway, as some of our guys had a better vantage point than me. They took the enemy out in a hail of fire, their less protected positions putting them at an extreme disadvantage.

The smoke cleared around the tanks, and one of them shoved the lead tank, which appeared to be immobilized, through the gap.

I jacked my Feemper up to full and tight and blasted at the second tank. It stopped for a moment, as if paralyzed, then moved again, rotating its turret towards our position.

"DOWN!" I yelled as a torrent of 20mm projectiles chipped away at the big rock behind which we took cover. Fortunately, they weren't high-explosive shells.

We rolled down and back. I heard the explosion of more RPG fire as the teams reloaded and let the tank have it.

"These guys have better armor than we thought," I head Jones pant into the com. "The tank we stopped just got free."

There was another buzz-saw rattle of 20mm fire and a tree near us exploded into splinters.

"Retreat!" I yelled. "Get back to better cover."

Ward and I took off for a position further down the hill, but the cover was thinning out.

"Dammit!" Ward said, as we ran. "If one of those tanks emerges from the brush, we're toast."

"There's a ditch coming up," I said. "Dive in."

We got down in the ditch and lay flat. I could see our other teams were still moving and with the GPS overlay it looked like they had some cover. The four other tanks had joined the first two and made it through the gap along with the rest of the enemy militia. Then I realized we were in deep shit, as I saw two of the minitanks and a team of four Axiosi infantry making their way down the hill to our position.

"They have us on their scanners," Ward said, reloading his RPG. "They'll be here in a minute."

"We can't take them," I said, as I watched our end appear. Pinned down in a ditch, what a way to go. Live by the sword...

"Fox!" Jock's voice came over my com. "You all right?"

"Hell no!" I yelled at him. "We have armor right on top of us! We're in a ditch, other side of the ridge."

"Help is on the way" Jock assured me. "Stay down!"

I felt the ground beneath me start to vibrate as the minitanks closed in.

"Is there a god of mercenaries?" Ward said. "I'd just like to know who to pray to."

"I don't think so," I said. "We're on our own."

BBBBBBBBRRRRRRRRRAAAAAAAAPPPPP!!! I heard the sound of a miniball cannon opening up, but it wasn't towards us!

A deafening sound of rockets filled the air and a huge shadow fell over us. There was the sound of plasma discharges, explosions and a few screams, and then there was silence. I glanced at my scanners and saw no enemy movement, so I ventured a glance over the edge of the ditch. Standing there in front of me was a massive Sfodrian knight, all alone amidst the wreckage and bodies of the tanks and men that had almost had our number. I checked my visor and saw nothing of the robot, then realized he must be completely shielded against scans.

The massive head of the knight rotated towards our position and I waved. He ignored me, then tucked himself into into a huge ball and rolled away from us, leaving a quarter-meter deep rut behind him.

"That was rude," Ward commented as we brushed ourselves off and got our bearings. I checked my screen for the rest of our men and saw the enemy had been immobilized and the rest of the squad we reforming about a tenth of a click from our position in the woods where we'd staged our ill-fated ambush. "I think I can forgive him, though."

"So long as he's shooting at the enemy and doesn't step on us, I don't care if he's the antichrist," I replied.

"You all right, Tommy? Ward?" Zelag's voice came over the com.

"A-okay," I replied. "Everybody good over there."

"Roger," he replied. "Knight bailed us out."

"Same here," I replied. "Nearing your position—there in two."

"Well, this was a total SNAFU," Ward said.

"Builds character," I said.

"Gets you killed unless you've got a giant killer robots in your pocket," Ward replied.

"There is that," I admitted. I shouldn't have approved an ambush with weapons not tested on the enemy. Just because the tanks were small, it didn't mean our RPGs were made for us. They were better weapons against trucks and transports, not tanks. Even minitanks, apparently. The important part of "live and learn" was the "live" part. And if I let the enthusiasm for battle take over my men without a good knowledge, I would get us killed. Every battlefield was different, every enemy was different, and we got thrown into new stuff all the time. I made a note to myself to exercise more caution in the future.

"Tommy!" Jones said, slapping me on the back. "You boys ran the wrong way out of the woods."

"Yeah, tell me about it," I said. "Realized too late we had almost no cover."

"We had 20mm fire incoming and would have been overrun in a moment," Ward said. "We made the only choice."

"We shouldn't have tried the ambush," I said.

"Why not?" Jones said. "Now we know RPGs and Feempers won't take down those little tanks. That's good intel."

"I'd rather not gather intel at the risk of my skull," I said. "Let some other idiot shoot at tanks and find out."

"The knights just smashed them like nothing," Ford said, waving towards the smoking and twisted remains of the tanks. "It was unbelievable."

"Tommy bring your men down," Jock said over the com. "All clear down here. We've got some captives, too. Couple of officers."

"All's well that ends well," Jones smiled. It was not a pretty sight.

As we rode back in the jeep, I found myself unable to dismiss a nagging thought. Four knights had come down and smashed up tanks and basically won the whole damn battle by themselves while we Wardogs, badasses though we be, didn't manage to accomplish much more than get overwhelmed by the enemy armor. I put my thoughts into words. "Guys, what the hell could possibly take out those knights?"

"Good question," Zelag said. "They shrugged off RPGs and 20mm cannon fire, small arms... they were practically invulnerable on the field."

"They don't even show up on scanners," Ward added. "Twenty feet tall and they're invisible!"

"Yeah," Jones added. "Gigantic invisible wrecking balls."

"So what could possibly take out a weapon like that?" I said. "Who *are* these mercenaries?

"We got the officers," Jones said, and winked. "I'll find out for you."

Chapter 7

Jones whistled a happy tune to himself as we prepared for the prisoners to reach the interrogation room. I tried not to think about the last time Jonesy found his happy place with a prisoner and a knife. Whatever it is that WDI screens out, it isn't psychopathy.

"Hey, Falkland," Edgerton said when he arrived. "I assumed you want Babbage to serve as our lie detector, so I took the liberty of setting him up for physiological scans and so forth." Edgerton held up a little silver scanner.

"Very good," I said. "We saved you the desk in the corner," I said. "You should put your helmet on, though."

"Why are we wearing our battlesuits?" he asked.

"Intimidation," I said. "We don't want them to see our faces."

"Yeah, and it's also because our armor scares the shit out of people," Jones added, lovingly studying the edge of a straight razor. "I wonder why?"

Jones, Ward, Edgerton and I were in a private warehouse WDI had rented for the occasion. Technically, the Sfodrians and Axiosi had a treaty that disallowed enhanced interrogation, but given the way their most highly-valued warriors were being lost, the Sfodrians only cared about the letter of the law. The niceties of a treaty from decades back weren't going to restrain them from saving their best, and if we took care of the details, they could also deny knowledge.

"Tommy, we got candidate number one ready," Zelag said over my com. "You ready?"

"The first prisoner is here," I told Jones. "You ready?"

"Always."

We flipped down our visors and Jones killed the lights, except for the spotlight over the "chair of misery", as he'd dubbed it. I think it was actually a gynecologist's chair to which he'd added some additional straps and spray-painted black, but "chair of misery" it was. Freaking Jones.

Zelag came in with a disoriented Axiosi officer in boxers and an undershirt. When the guy saw the chair, his eyes widened and he started to struggle, but Ward and Jones easily tied him down thanks to their servo-powered suits.

"I shot him up with some strong stuff," Zelag said over the com so the prisoner couldn't hear him. "He shouldn't remember any of this. The Sfodrians might just shoot him or they might let him go, but one of them told me to be careful about leaving too many marks just in case."

"Low energy," Jones said, shaking his head and picking up the razor again, then setting it down mournfully. "How is a guy supposed to put in a good day's work under these conditions? We need a union."

"It's mostly psychology anyhow," Zelag said. "You don't really need to carve your initials in his spleen with a rusty pocketknife to get what you need."

"You don't understand art," Jones said. "It's not always about what's necessary."

"Get to it, Jonesey," I told him. "Enough foreplay."

Less than a kilosec later, the officer was ready to talk. It was a smart move on his part as Jones was starting to get bored and he got considerably more creative when he was bored.

"Grachev," he finally admitted. "They're from Grachev!"

"Grachev?" I said over the com. I'd never heard of the place. "What's that?"

"It's a planet on the edges of the Man-Machine Unity," Edgerton said. "It's under Unity control."

"Jones, ask guy dude what their mercenary friends look like," I said.

"Describe your buddies from Grachev," Jones ordered.

"I didn't see much of them," the officer pleaded. "I swear!"

Jones stepped a little closer. "It's the truth," the guy said quickly. "You can't see much of them. They keep covered up for the most part. You know, in their suits."

"For the most part?" Jones said. "Tell us what you know about the lesser part."

"I didn't actually see them myself. But there's another officer who told me he saw their eyes once when a flash from an explosion lit up the merc's faceplate from the side."

"So, what about it?" Jones said.

"And he said the guy's eyes looked silver."

"That proves nothing," Ward muttered. "Could just be medical implants. A cam augment, maybe. Enhanced vision."

I thought back to Betty's wide-spaced silver eyes. Eye replacements weren't all that common, but it didn't necessarily mean someone was a true cyborg. But then, the mercs were from a Unity-dominated world.

"Silver eyes," Jones said. "Anything else?"

"No," the officer said firmly.

"That's not enough," Jones said. "Think harder!"

The man was quiet for a moment, then spoke. "I know one more thing. They talk weird."

"How so?"

"Just weird. I don't know. Not like us."

"Dammit," Jones said. "Do I need to take your ears off just to get you to pay attention?"

"No," the man said. "No, it's just... they're just different! Real cold and direct. Precise. Everything they do and say is, I don't know, efficient, I guess." He blinked a few times and started to slouch in the chair.

"We're not going to get much more out of him," Ward said.

"That's enough for now," I decided. "Put him under and we'll talk to the other guy. Zelag, get him out of here."

We worked on the other guy for a while and didn't get much more, though the second officer said he was convinced the mercenaries had prosthetic arms, as he'd seen one of them get injured by a knight and lose a chunk of his armor. The merc had wires and tubing up his forearms, with strange fingers that looked like some sort of silvery alloy. Edgerton's AI confirmed the man was telling the truth and we sent him back to his cell with a much better idea of what we were facing. It wasn't certain, but there was enough evidence for us to pin them down as cyborgs, which meant they were almost certainly Unity. We had a pretty good idea what they were, and now we needed to learn was how they were taking out the 6-meter-tall robotic wrecking balls that ruled Sfodria.

A group of us gathered around the console the Sfodrians had linked to my retina and I searched for more video footage of mercenary attacks. At first I came up with nothing, then realized the paranoid Sfodrians had censored the search results. After a talk with Yost and Pitt explaining our need for more intel, they got in touch with the Lord General's technicians and I was granted access. Not only that, but the Stratocracy techs even provided us with the data they'd collected from the knight's onboard black box systems. These gathered biometric data, external temperatures, scanner results, and, best of all, suitcam video footage. We gathered together again and I started my analysis anew. Each knight had an array of cameras built into his armor, providing a variety of views. It took me a while to figure out how to identify the various views, switch between them, and determine out what I was seeing, but I eventually figured it out. The Sfodrian interface was all symbol-based, which was initially confusing, but also prevented any problems with their unique terminology.

"There's some footage that looks interesting," Ward said over my shoulder, pointing out a cluster of small animated circles displaying terrain, nested in a list of results. I pulled one of them up and was greeted by the sight of weeds being trampled by massive feet.

"That's the wrong cam," Zelag helpfully observed.

"Zip it, Cyborg," I snapped, looking for another view. I found one and we were greeted by the sight of a flat, dusty terrain flying past at a good 60 kph. Judging by the altitude of the view, the camera was built into the knight's helmet. Flashes of red-purple plasma blasts suddenly appeared in the view and the image jerked rapidly from side to side, until it zoomed in on a pair of armored figures with rifles. I saw the huge laser sword slash past and the flash as pulses of energy destroyed the attackers—and then the view flashed white for a moment under what I assumed was more incoming from another angle. The view shifted again and we saw a figure in black appear on the lower left of the screen, rifle raised. There was a flash from the muzzle.

"That's a projectile!" Ward said excitedly. "Axiosi regulars have plasma."

The sword swung around to strike the threat, glowing with white-hot plasma, and then the image broke up into flashing incoherent red symbols and static before going completely blank.

"That's the end of the footage," I said.

"Nothing more?" Zelag asked.

"That's it for that one. We can try another view." I looked for another camera and found one which aimed down the knight's huge robotic right arm. The glowing sword was front and center.

"Kill cam!" Jones said.

We watched as the same scenes repeated. The two Axiosi blasted to bits, the turn toward the other threat, then a glimpse of the attacked followed by a view of the sky, then nothing.

"That was from Sir Arhaxtus," I said, looking though the information alongside the footage. "Killed two weeks ago. According to the rest of the data here, he lost contact with base and was found blown to pieces later that day. No enemy in the area when they picked up his body."

"Find another attack," Jones said, so I did, looking up the final moments of Sir Metaxis.

This time I got the helmet cam the first time and watched as the knight effortlessly dispatched a platoon of Axiosi regulars and a tank before his screens suddenly busted into digital confetti and went blank.

"See if we can see what hit him," Zelag said, so I switched through cameras. This time we spotted an enemy soldier firing from behind him. The method of attack was the same. It looked like a projectile weapon of some sort, then the knight hit the ground seconds later with all his systems knocked out.

"Some sort of Feemper?" Jones said. "Maybe a make and model we haven't seen?"

"No way," Zelag replied. "First, Feempers aren't projectile weapons. And second, these knights are freaking shielded like you wouldn't believe. I spent some time going over what I could find in Pitt's files. You could set off a nuke at their feet and they'd survive."

"It's just a little projectile, though," Jones said. "Taking out something like these guys with a slug-thrower is crazy."

"You mean impossible. It's got to be more than simple slugs," I said.

"How about nanotech?" Ward suggested.

"You think?" Jones said. "Like, maybe they hit the knight with a blast of creepy crawlies and they burrow in and toast him?"

"Sure," Zelag said, nodding. "That would make sense. The armor is made for stopping real firepower, plasma, slugs, EMP, whatever. It's probably not designed to keep out a sufficiently hardened nanite penetrator."

"That stuff is seriously illegal," Jones said, making a dubious face.

"Who's gonna enforce it?" I said. "This is a League planet. The TA isn't going to interfere. It's possible, if you assume these mercs are playing by different rules."

"Yeah, but what are they after?" Jones said. "Why would some cyborg freaks—no offense, Zee—show up and start randomly blasting some knights, knocking out some factories and helping some ass-backwards world. I thought they considered themselves as some sort of god-machines above all of us mortals?"

"None taken," Zelag said, with a grin. "That's what I've heard too. And if they're gearing up to start another war to take control of the galaxy away from humanity, this is a very strange way to go about it."

"We can worry about their motives later," I said. "I think we've at least found how they're knocking out the knights."

I pulled up another kill from the previous week and it was the same thing. This time we didn't see the shooter, but the black box was abruptly fried in the middle of combat and we got to see a pretty dramatic faceplant that was followed by static.

"I just can't believe they're able to take out these bad boys so easily," Jones said. "That's some seriously evil gear they've got."

"Yeah," Zelag said. "And what if it works on our battlesuits?"

There was a moment of silence. None of us were particularly happy to think about the possible consequences of that.

"Anyhow, we need to talk to the Sfodrians about this," I said.

"That'll be fun," Ward said. "I'm sure they'll enjoy hearing a commoner tell them how easily their superheroes go down."

"We don't get paid for nothing."

"Sure," Zelag said, drumming his robotic fingers on the desk, "but I think we should do something else before we go and tell them that the weapons and hereditary aristocracy that are the foundation of their entire society are helpless."

"Like what?" I asked, shutting down the console in front of me.

"I wouldn't go in with news like that without some sort of a proposal that at least provides some hope of a solution. We are the experts, right? We were brought in here because they're desperate. We don't want to make them even more desperate. Forget getting paid, they could go on a society-wide suicidal dive and take us with them."

"Well, what are we supposed to tell them?" Jones said. "It's true. They send out a big freaking robot guy to kick ass and five seconds later he's laying tits up on the grass after some Unity freak hits him with a single lovetap. We don't use nanites ourselves, and the locals don't have it, so we just have to tell them the truth. They're toast."

"No," Zelag said. "We don't just tell them they're toast. We don't even know that's true. They're the client, they need to believe we're worth what they're paying us. We've got some of the best, smartest researchers in the spinward sectors to call upon. So what we do, my dear brothers-in-arms, is we get our guys working on a solution before we even let them know about the problem. It's not like they're expecting us to have figured this out already, right?"

"Yeah," I said, standing up and stretching. "Let's at least try to sound smart. How about you talk to Pitt and get him to start some guys working on a solution? Edgerton, for one."

"And get us some better food while you're there," Jones said. "I'm about to eat my mattress."

"I'm on it," Zelag said. "What about you?"

"I'll see if Yost will get me an audience with the Lord General. I'll tell him we're already working on a solution and see if we can stop them from throwing any more knights against the Axiosi until we've got a way to shield them."

"That'll go over like a lead balloon," Zelag said. "But you're right. They're probably losing a billion credits every time a knight goes down, not to mention the human loss. Good luck."

"You too," I said, then headed for Yost's office.

"I put Corporal Falkland and his team in charge of investigating the situation on the ground, Lord General," Captain Yost said. "We've analyzed the data concerning the unprecedented losses of your knights and have concluded that you are facing a very urgent threat that requires an immediate modification of your military strategy. Corporal, take it from here."

Lord General Landros glowered at me with his human eye and probably shot me with x-rays from his cybernetic one. We were meeting him in a thick-walled round room called the Chamber of Meetings, along with five well-built men in formal suits that did nothing to conceal their extremely muscular frames. Each suit had a different color scheme and a different insignia on the left breast pocket. I assumed they were knights, but the Lord General did not introduce them. Their eyes bored into me as I stood next to Yost.

"So?" Landros said, turning to me. "Speak!"

"The knights need to be benched for the time being," I said. I'm sure a WDI sales rep would have come up with a less upsetting way to say that, but my job is to break things and kill people, not make people happy. And man, they were not happy.

"How dare you?" one of the audience roared. He was a red-faced silver-haired guy with a streaked Fu-Manchu that reached his chest. "We are the soul and the strength of the state!"

"These mercenary offworlders seek to worm their way in and force us to rely on them rather than our own arms!"

"Ignoble soldiers-of-fortune!"

"Honorless whores!"

Yep, pretty sure they were knights.

"Noble sirs," Yost broke in, holding up his hands. "We were brought here to help you defeat your ancestral enemy. Perhaps you might let Corporal Falkland explain what he has learned before tearing him to pieces."

The five nobles all glared at him, but they did quit sniping at me as they fell into an angry silence.

"Continue please, Corporal," Yost ordered once the room fell silent.

I stayed cool and returned the furious stares without blinking. "They have found a way to neutralize your strength, and that makes your state vulnerable."

"Through cowardly ambushes and technological toys," one of the knights sneered.

"Yes," I agreed. "Anyone in their right mind would be terrified of your awesome capabilities. But it is because of their unwillingness to face you directly in honorable battle that they have found a way to take you down. Have you ever lost so many knights in such a short time before?"

"Never," the Lord General growled.

"Exactly," I replied. "That's because you have never faced the Unity."

"The Unity?" the silver-haired knight with the beard said. "The alien mutants?"

"Yes," I agreed. "Those alien mutants are working with the Axiosi, and your men are getting killed because they brought with them an alien nanotechnology your suits are unable to combat at this time."

That shut them up. They looked at each other, and for the first time I saw something that looked suspiciously like alarm penetrate the Lord General's unshakeable arrogance.

"Can they truly neutralize our armor?" questioned a dark-haired knight whose suit was red and brown. On his breast was the insignia of a skull pierced by an axe.

"Without question," I said. "We are working on the tech aspect already. I am not telling you that your equipment is obsolete, I am only recommending that you stop putting yourselves at risk until the vulnerability can be resolved."

"We are not afraid to die," declared the silver-haired knight. "You commoners cannot understand honor."

"That's as may be," I said. "But even if you're willing to die, are you willing to leave the state without defense?"

"It is always better to die with honor than to cower in fear of facing the enemy on the field," another knight shouted. But judging by their expressions, his fellows did not seem quite as convinced that pointless death was a reasonable objective.

"Are you certain that these aliens are using unlawful nanotechnology?" said the silver-haired knight. "Can you prove it?"

"Have you not watched any of the armor cams from the men you've lost?"

"We do not think about defeat," said the guy in red and brown. "Our focus is only, and always, on victory!"

I sighed. No wonder they couldn't figure out a counter to the enemy's action. "Well, it is our philosophy that knowledge of defeat is the way to find new paths to victory. What is happening is that your knights are being fired upon by an advanced projectile weapon of some kind, after which their computer systems are rapidly compromised and their energy shields fail."

"How does this prove a nanotechnology attack?" the Lord General demanded.

"It doesn't prove it," I admitted. "But in our well-informed opinion, it is the most logical conclusion."

"Then we fight," said the silver-haired man. "Come back to us when you can offer us proof that our valor is certain to be in vain."

"Thank you, Captain, Corporal. I pronounce this audience to be at an end," the Lord General said, and he indicated the door with his hand.

Captain Yost glanced at me, we both nodded our respects to the Lord General and his knights, and we departed the room. Behind us, the chamber's thick metal door slammed shut with a resounding boom. I knew it would serve as the death knell of many a knight, likely including some in that room, if we could not provide them with an answer soon.

Chapter 8

Someone kicked my cot.

"Drop your cocks and pick up your socks!" shouted a familiar voice. "It's reveille!"

"Squid?" I said, sitting up and rubbing at my eyes. "Whaddup?"

"Enemy troops moving in on Phalix, a town about 300 clicks from here in the foothills of the Makken range."

I nodded and pulled on my shirt, then popped the latch on the case where my armor was stowed. "Why do we care?" Ward grunted, as he quickly went through a few of his morning stretches, then pulled out his own armor.

"Some sort of important manufacturing site there, something to do with the knight's armor," Squid said. "Get your asses to the field right away, we've got an air transport in about a kilosec. Breakfast in the air."

"Great," Ward said, locking his chest plate into place. "I'll fight anyone to get away from that fishy stuff."

My head felt fuzzy. I'd spent a long evening with Edgerton and Morrel, scanning once more through all the video we could find from battles where knights were lost. We didn't get any detailed shots of the mercs in any of them, and the feed-ending kill shots we did see were delivered by guys that looked just like the rest of the Axiosi regulars. Whether they were cyborged inhumans or not, there was no obvious difference on the field.

We had called it quits at around one. I checked my chronometer. It was 0462 now and there was no time to brew anything up. I locked

my helmet into place and took a quick hit of stim from the banks
in my battlesuit and my mind cleared. One of the docs had told
me RockMed was our new drug contractor on the suit meds. The
stimulant was effective enough, but its instantaneous results lacked
the restorative effect of a morning ritual.

"Hey, what happened to my chocolate?" Ward asked, rooting
around in his rucksack.

"I ate it," I said.

"Dammit, Tommy," he said. "You owe me!"

We headed to the field. When we arrived, about half the platoon
was already there. The sky above was cloudy as we stood beneath the
ugly blue-white of the massive overhead lights that lit the gritty surface
of the landing area. Palm-sized insects with white wings and long,
feathery tails circled the lights. Just another early morning on another
strange planet, fighting people we didn't know for people we didn't
like.

At least we got paid well.

Ace arrived and thumped me on the shoulder. "Hey Falkland, you
having fun playing scientist?"

"Hardly," I said. "It takes a lot of time to learn very little, and then
they go ahead and shoot us down anyhow."

"Just be glad you're not a pilot," Ace laughed. "If I get shot down, I
die."

"Fair enough," I said. "You flying us out today?"

"I wish," he said. "We've got a Sfodrian transport on the way.
Some local make. I got no valid certs here and they're sticklers for
credentials."

"Too bad," I said. "I'd trust a Wardog without certs over a local with
50,000 hours."

"Tell me about it," he agreed.

I looked around and counted twenty-three Wardogs, some holding
their helmets, others with visors up. Those would get flipped down
when locals showed but at the moment we were alone.

The sound of a jeep buzzed in my ears and I saw Yost in his dress uniform and Squid in his battlesuit ride up behind us, trailed by two other jeeps filled with Pitt and some of the WDI support guys. We locked our visors and helmets down as the jeeps were followed by a ground transport full of Sfodrian militia. A couple more jeeps showed up over the next couple of minutes, and the ground crew finally lit the hangar and tower lights. From what I'd heard, this was minor militia base; it certainly lacked the professionalism we'd seen from the knights.

"All right, boys," Squid said, calling us together. "Captain Yost and I have gone over the objectives. We're headed to Phalix to defend a mission-critical manufacturing facility. There is currently a Sfodrian garrison there which we will support and advise. The platoon will be divided into three squads. Sergeant Hanley will lead Green, I've got Gold and Corporal Falkland will lead Blue. Green and Gold squads will embed with the militia and provide tactical advice and muscle as needed. Blue will act as a tactical reserve, and will be equipped with L-24s. Based on what we've learned, we believe the mercenaries are targeting the knights with some sort of nano-weapon. Tommy, your team is to watch for these bastards and knock 'em down. Defend the knights at all costs, and let's see if we can grab one of those weapons if we can!"

The sound of throbbing antigrav fields made it to my ears as a large gray transport approached and landed in the field.

"There's our ride, men," Squid said. "It's go time."

We divided into our three squads and marched onto the transport. I recognized it as an A-67, albeit a stripped-down model, that was painted a somber gray and marked with the image of a fist grasping a handful of sticks.

We were followed by the Sfodrian militia guys, many of whom looked like as if they'd been dragged right from their beds and dumped off here. They gave us plenty of space, staring at our armor with a mixture of curiosity and fear. They were obviously not a company that had worked with any of our guys before. Once we were airborne, a Sfodrian militia overseer briefed his men on the situation and explained our presence, letting them know that we were "noble allies of Sfodria" here to "help keep them alive as good servants" so they could continue to work "for the glory of the state".

I gripped my Feemper and tried not to think about the situation. I took a deep breath and tried to let the tension of upcoming battle roll through me and wash away. Defending the knights was something we had to do, but as I sat in the belly of that throbbing A-67, I began to concoct a plan of my own.

I brought up the tactical overlay on my display. The enemy was in the foothills only a few clicks away from the LZ. Green and Gold Squads had connected with the militia while I led Blue Squad along the railway tracks parallel to the rolling hills where we assumed the knights would most likely engage the enemy. We could hear the thumping of scattered mortar fire hitting the town behind us.

"They'd better knock out those mortars," Edgerton said. "They're going to break everything we're trying to save."

"They're on it," Ward replied, pointing to a flight of drones soaring overhead.

"Why aren't we seeing more activity in the sky?" Jones said.

"It's some sort of old treaty," Zelag said. "Don't you read the briefings?"

"Why bother when I have you to do it for me?" Jones replied.

"Zip it," I told them. "Red is on the move."

My visor displayed Wardogs in blue, enemy units in red, with Sfodrian friendlies in green. The Sfodrians had a few fortified positions on the edge of the city behind us, but the garrison had been bunched up in a vulnerable position in the open space in front of us. Our guys must have convinced their officers to take better positions, because I could see they'd now spread out and settled into some of the higher ground.

I saw the Axiosi moving towards us now, and I noted they were taking the path we'd anticipated. My tactical overlay showed their armor was position towards the front with some mobile artillery behind the infantry. The drones were harrying the artillery, taking out the occasional cannon, but a few of them were being knocked down by tracking lasers.

"There are a lot of guys coming in," Ward said. "They might walk right through those militia. It's a pretty even match numbers-wise and the Sfodrians are in no shape to hold their ground."

"They've got Wardogs with 'em now," Jones said. "Squid and Jock'll stiffen their spines."

"Or shoot a few of them as examples," I said, then saw something worrying on my tactical display. "Hey, is anyone getting ghosting off to the right of your tac-screen. Like something might be moving into range?"

"Not seeing it," Ward said. "No—wait—yeah, something blipped there for a sec, then nothing."

"Probably jamming," Jones said.

"Jamming usually covers everything in range, not just specific troops," Edgerton said. "I'll bet it's some sort of advanced cloaking."

"If that's the Unity bastards, they're going to run into us about the same time the Axiosi regulars come through," I said. "Let's move forward so we can hit them sooner and disrupt their schedule. Keep your heads down; we don't want them to spot us if their scanners haven't picked us up yet."

Some of us got behind rocks and others took cover in an old block building by the railroad tracks. The ghost on the display popped in and out a few times. I entered the building by kicking in a rusty door and found a convenient window facing the direction where I thought the cloaked units would appear.

"Squid, Falkland here," I told him. "I know we're supposed to wait for the knights, but we've got a situation developing here." The ghostly blur appeared again closer than I had expected. Damn, those Unity guys were moving fast.

"Copy that, Corporal. What's the problem."

"Looks like we have some cloaked mercs moving towards us. We're going to bushwhack them, then join up with the knights."

"I copy. Good luck, Tommy. Over."

"What is it, Tommy?" Zelag said, pulling me back to the moment.

"We're going to ambush them, catch ourselves a cyborg, then drag him back with us. No more guessing. If we're lucky, we'll catch him alive and talk to the freak ourselves."

"Sounds good to me," Jones said.

"They must be hunting the knights, right?" I said. "So, how about we give the research guys some source material and grab some intel of our own."

"That sounds fine with me," Morrel said.

"Feemper might straight-up kill a cyborg," Jones said.

"Yeah, but it might not," I said. "We'll just do our best. Just cover the knights first."

"It would help if we actually knew where they were," Ward muttered. "Arrogant bastards won't even share a com."

"Don't bitch about the clients," Zelag said. "They're paying us."

"Hey—there it is," Waterose said.

I saw it too. The entire tactical display on my screen was blurring out.

"Wide-array jammers," Ward said. "We don't have anything that strong that's man-portable!"

Our tech was solid. The tactical overlays had saved us more than once, but militaries are always staying on top of tech. You invent better armor, they invent better guns. You invent a faster drone, they invent a faster anti-drone laser array. With Pyrrha's tech level, I thought we might be able to rely on our displays, but it was obvious that the two sides had anticipated tactical scanning and created countermeasures for it. "Back to the stone age," I said, turning off the tactical overlay. "Eyes open for the cloaks."

As dismaying as the blackout felt, the fact was that losing our tactical imaging was probably a net plus for our guys. Wardogs were accustomed to fighting under all tech levels and conditions and with both sides being jammed, which meant we would be able to move around more easily without being seen. Heck, if I didn't know better, I might have thought Captain Yost called for the blackout.

The ground started to shake—I looked around to see what was causing it—then saw a flash of green and silver tear past our position, followed by another in orange and black.

"Knights!" Edgerton yelled. "There they are!"

The cloaked units weren't the mercs, they were the knights! The tactical situation suddenly made more sense.

"Follow them!" I ordered, and we ran from our positions to follow the rolling behemoths. I watched as the first two went tearing down through the field towards the rear of the Sfodrian militia. We couldn't keep up, but our armor made us almost twice as fast as an unassisted runner. As we ran to follow the knights, three more came up from behind us, zipping around us. A strange voice came over my com, haughty and cold. "You are not in your prearranged position. Are you lost, Thomas?"

"Who is this?" I replied. "Get off the comm!"

Another huge robotic form rolled past me, this one in red and brown.

"Just passed you, mercenary," the voice said.

I was talking to a knight. I wondered if it might be that guy in red and brown from the other night. Actually, if he was willing to talk, that could be useful, even if he was just taunting me.

"I don't know how you got my com, sir, but we are at your service," I said, showing a damn big pile of restraint.

"It is unnecessary," the knight said, then the com cut out. Jackass. I stored the incoming ID so I could talk suit-to-suit with the guy again if the need arose. The knight was already 500 meters in front of me.

We got in view of the battle and I saw the enemy, their combined arms mostly obscured by smoke. "Hold up here for a moment, men," I ordered. We were hopelessly behind the knights. Flashes of plasma and pulse grenades lit the whole mess from the inside. The knights were taking places inside the Sfodrian militia, like massive artillery towers. I saw six on the field already, with another six moving in from the west, firing pulses of fire into the Axiosi position. I couldn't make much sense of the fighting but it looked like our guys had directed the Sfodrians to split up into a main body and a couple of fast flanking units—the incoming Axiosi looked to be getting sucked in to a "U" of Sfodrian units.

"Double envelopment," Waterose said needlessly.

It looked like the knights and militia were cleaning up the enemy. We needed to get down there and hunt a cyborg. So far, all the knights were up and seemed to be doing fine. Heck, maybe the Unity wasn't even involved in this attack and we were on a wild goose chase. I would have thought they'd strike by now. "Let's get down there," I said, and we took off towards the knights. As we got closer, I turned my tactical overlay on again. Most of it was dark, except now I could see the signatures of my fellow War-dogs. From looking at the field and viewing their positions, I could see how the militia had managed to flank and pin the Axiosi down. Now with the knights behind them, throwing down blasts of plasma and massive missile strikes in all directions, it was looking like the fight would be over before we got down to the field.

"Falkland, I've got visual on you," came Squid's voice. "What happened to that ambush?"

"The cloaked units were friendly."

"You're far behind the knights."

"Affirmative," I said. "They didn't wait for us, Sarge."

"No harm, no foul," Squid replied. "Just get down here as fast as you can and you can help us clean up."

By the time we got to the field, the battle was mostly over. The remaining enemy units were pulling back to a defensible position and our guys were standing in the midst of a field of smoking machinery and dead bodies. I hadn't even fired a single shot.

"Welcome to the party," Jock said, meeting up with us. "You see any mercs out in the woods?"

"No," I replied. "Looks like you guys didn't either."

"We'll search the corpses," Jock said. "We still might find one."

A dozen Sfodrian knights formed up into a circle about 100 meters from our position.

"What are they doing?" Jock asked.

"Beats me," I said, watching the twelve lift their massive swords and light them with plasma. Then, to my surprise, they took off towards the enemy position, leaving their troops behind.

"Dammit," I said. "Looks like they're taking on the enemy alone—hey—you got a jeep?" I looked around and saw one parked beside a shattered tree stump.

"No keys," Jock said.

"Edgerton," I said, moving to the vehicle. "Can you start this piece of junk."

"On it," he said, running over to our position and sitting in the jeep. He studied the dash, then reached under the seat and pulled out a tool kit, dug around, then smashed something into the dash and started making adjustments.

"He's a natural carjacker," Jones said approvingly.

"Jones, Ward, Zelag—come on," I said. "We're following those knights. The rest of you stay with Jock here."

The jeep started. "These models are all simple chip-driven," Edgerton said with a grin. "All I had to do was—"

"Shut up, Edgerton," I explained, as I jumped into the jeep with the others and gunned it towards the knights. I watched as the enemy lay down a barrage of fire upon them and they shrugged it off as if it was nothing, laying down arcs of plasma into the retreating enemy.

"Hey Sir Robot," I said, trying the com signal of the knight. "You have a death wish or something?"

There was no reply for a moment, then the com opened. "It is they who wish to die, Thomas," he said. "We're simply helping them along. Why are you following us?"

"I have orders," I replied. "It's our duty." I could see the red and brown knight now, pursuing a squad of enemy soldiers in the company of the silver and green knight. I swerved to avoid a fallen soldier and almost nailed a boulder, then jerked back and overcompensated, fishtailing the vehicle. I got it back under control just in time to be thrown in the air by an explosion. *THUMP!* I went flying through the air head over heels, glimpsing purple skies then yellow grit as I slammed face-first into the ground. "Tommy!" came Ward's voice as I blinked and got my bearings. Suit readout showed I hadn't broken anything, but my shoulder hurt like hell. "We hit something!"

"Hit what, a knight?" I said, regaining my feet. I looked and saw Jones and Zelag rising to their feet. Ward was already at my side. The jeep was wrecked.

"RPG?" I looked around, shaking my head, but I didn't figure it out before a plasma bolt ablated on my thigh armor. I felt the area heat up briefly as I dropped to the ground. "Ambush! Get down!"

Ward and I crawled behind a boulder and he returned fire towards the enemy. I felt cooling topical anesthetic ease the fire from my injured leg and looked down at my armor. It was seared towards the inner thigh. Checking my vitals on the visor, it looked like I could still move. "I'm counting a dozen of them," Jones growled over the com as he laid down suppressive fire. "Zelag is moving to your position. Keep him covered!"

We opened up with our Feempers on plasma as Zelag rushed over to our rocky sanctuary. A few bolts of plasma zipped past him but he made it.

"Go, Jones, go! We'll cover you!"

The enemy were firing from behind a ruined wall. We blasted away at them and forced them to take cover as Jones ran towards us, but then one of them lobbed a grenade that hit the ground behind him and exploded, throwing him into the air. *BOOM!* He went flying tail over tea-kettle, hurled towards us by the force of the blast. I saw an enemy head pop up behind the wall and blew it off with my Feemper on full plasma, an explosion of red showing I'd found my target. Ward and I kept firing, suppressing them as Zelag ran out and dragged Jones to our position.

"Jones," I shouted, noting his dented helmet and cracked visor. "Talk to me!"

Jones mumbled something about horses. Or maybe whores. It didn't make sense, but at least he was alive.

"Come on, Jonesy!" I said. "Pull it together!"

Another grenade rolled past and we hunkered down as it harmlessly blasted a stand of cactus into green jelly. I wiped some of the cactus juice off my visor and linked my chip to Jones's suit. Helmet integrity down to 65 percent and his status indicated a probable concussion. BOOM! Another blast off to our right announced the enemy had launched another grenade. Plasma fire started to come in at more of an angle and I realized the enemy was trying to flank us.

"Jones!" I tried again, trying to hold him up against the rock.

"Tommy," he mumbled. "I hit my head."

"You tried to fly, dude. Hang in there, we need to keep them from getting round us."

"Squid!" I said. "This is Fox. We're pinned down! You reading our suits from there?"

"I got nothing," came the reply. "Where are you?"

I checked my suit GPS but got nothing. Jammers were still active.

"We headed towards the knights—another couple of clicks towards the enemy position from you. Any eyes in the sky?"

"Negative on that," Squid replied. "Drones were neutralized. We'll see if we can reach you—sit tight."

Another explosion threw chunks of rock over Jones and me, as I held him up. "Damn head injuries," he mumbled. "Always with the head injuries. Wanna get a diffrent injury sometime, jes for helluvit."

"Shut up, Jones," I said as a bolt of plasma lit a briar tree on fire behind me. "Lie flat here. We need to relieve the pressure."

"We're totally pinned," Ward said, as he and Zelag crouched behind the rock. "They're hitting us from ten, twelve and two. They'll be at our sides in a moment, then we're toast."

"So first we take out two, then force them to retreat. Ward, you fire all your grenades at ten, then suppress twelve on full-auto. Zee, you and me will rush two and take them out. Off the chain in 3... 2... 1!"

I was trusting in surprise and our superior armor. It had worked many times before, after all. But the scorched mark on my thigh was a reminder that despite our battlesuits, we were not invulnerable. Zee and I charged as Ward launched a small hailstorm of grenades in the opposite direction, then spun and began hosing down the enemies in the middle.

Zee launched his grenades as we ran, but I saved mine. We got about halfway there before the Axiosi recovered from the initial blasts, but they were shaken and fired their initial shots too quickly. Nothing came close to either of us, and I took the opportunity to launch a salvo of my own grenades. FOOMP-FOOMP-FOOMP-FOOMP-FOOMP-FOOMP!

I felt my left arm piston like a machine as the mini-grenades were fired out of the forearm launcher, and the Axiosi fire stopped abruptly just before there were six sizable explosions barely 30 meters in front of us. Zee had gotten ahead of me, so I kicked in the servos and we covered the remaining distance in about 15 seconds. We were almost to the low, rocky rise behind which the Axiosi were positioned when one of them popped up and fired his laser right at Zee, hitting him in the arm. That was his last act, as I leaped forward and drove my armored fist right through his helmeted skull, popping the steel and bone as if it were a balloon.

Zee cursed angrily and leaped over the barrier, and kicked the only remaining survivor about ten meters backward into a rock. There was a loud crack and the guy slumped to the ground, though I didn't know if he was dead or just unconscious. I looked around. Between the grenades and our plasma cannons, the unarmored enemy platoon had been either blown to bits, incinerated, or in some cases, a little of both.

"You all right?"

Zee nodded. "Shorted out my arm for a second there, but it's back online now. How are Ward and Jonesy holding up?"

We looked back. Judging by the amount of plasma being hurled back and forth from their position, it appeared they were doing all right.

"We need to move on those guys to our right," I observed.

"Sure," Zelag agreed. "But we just used up all our grenades, so what are you thinking?"

Just as I was about to reply, a massive sweep of purple energy flew over our heads and struck the enemy position we were considering. The fire being directed at Ward and Jonesey came to an abrupt halt. The ground shook as massive footsteps approached and a massive robotic wrecking ball laid down concentrated whoopass on the enemy.

"Need a little help, Warpuppies?" came the voice of the red-and-brown knight over my com.

"Much obliged," I told him without a shred of sarcasm. The enemy fire dropped off us and concentrated on the knight, not that it did them any good. The knight towered above the battlefield like a statue erected to the god of war, and was joined by his friend in green and silver. The two of them blasted away at the last enemy position, before rushing forward and chasing them out from their cover. I'll admit it, I laughed when I saw the silver-and-green knight step on a brave, but doomed soldier who stood his ground and blasted desperately upward at the mighty mechawarrior.

"Go on home, outworlder," the knight told me. "This is our sandbox. We do not need you to help us play in it."

I didn't think we had done so badly for ourselves, but I could see his point.

"All right," I said to my team. "We've got a man down and the knights seem to be taking care of themselves. Let's meet up with Squid."

"I think we should–" Ward said, then stopped. "Wait—what?" The silver-and-green knight had suddenly stopped moving about eighty meters to our left. I watched as he fell to the ground and was swarmed by a squad of the enemy, blasting into the chinks of his armor. The massive warrior didn't even raise an arm to stop them—and then I watched as a man stood on top of his chest and pushed something into where his helmet met his neck. "Holy hell," Ward said, as the men jumped away from the knight. Seconds later, there was the CRACK of an explosion and the knight's head was blown apart from his body, rolling a good ten meters before coming to a halt. I looked around for the knight in red and brown and saw him to our right, running towards his fallen fellow.

"Enemy mercs have to be around here somewhere. That knight just froze up without warning!" I said. "Ward, we gotta nail them. Set your rifle for max EMP, no plasma, tight focus. Sit tight, Jonesy. Zee, you stay with him. We don't want to fry your arm again."

I switched my rifle from plasma to EMP assist and we sprinted after the surviving knight. His sword was blazing bright and he was blasting away at the enemy as they retreated from the giant metal corpse of his fellow. It looked like he was going to rout them easily, until an enemy soldier appeared out of nowhere and shot him with one of those weird rifles we'd seen on the black box footage.

"There's the bastard!" I yelled, and we opened fire on the unsuspecting mercenary. The combination of the twin EMP pulses dropped him to the ground, smoking. But it was already too late! The knight staggered, took one unsteady step, then fell flat on his face.

"We have to cover him," I shouted. "Switch back to plasma." We took cover behind the huge body of the fallen knight. "Yo, Sir

Flat-On-His-Face," I said over the knight's channel. "You alive in there?"

"Yes, Thomas," came the reply. "But my systems appear to be entirely nonfunctional."

"We nailed the guy that hit you," I said. A bolt of plasma zipped over my head. "We're covering you. Can't you move at all?"

"No. Nothing is responding," the knight replied, his voice now crackling with static. "And there is a pain in my head."

"You're losing your coms too," I said, firing a shot that took down a charging Axiosi. "How do we get you out of there?" There was no reply except for a hiss of static like waves rolling up on a beach.

"Falkland," Jock said over the com. "I'm seeing a fallen knight here. Is that near your position?"

"What color?" I said.

"Orange and black."

"No, that's not him!" I replied, opening up on two more Axiosi and sending them scurrying back into the brush. "Look for Ward and I camped out behind the fallen body of a knight in red and brown. And blast the everliving shit out of the enemy with your EMP on max or else whatever knights are remaining won't be standing long. Knight over here just got his head blown clean off. Looks like the Unity are embedded with the regulars. They look like everyone else, but they seem to be keeping themselves cloaked until they have a shot."

"Roger," Jock said. "We're all moving in your direction. Just sit tight."

My leg started to throb and I dialed in an analgesic to take the edge off. It felt like the pain was inside the muscle now. I looked for a target, then realized the firing around us was dying down. I looked back towards Sfodrian-controlled territory and saw a group of militia moving forward with three Wardogs in their midst. "Well, Fox," came Squid's voice over the com. "You boys decided to bag yourselves a knight, eh?"

"You could say that," I said, then pointed towards the rock where Zelag and Jones were positioned. "Other half of my team is over there. Jones is down with a concussion."

"Looks like you took a hit yourself," Squid said, coming forward and noticing my leg.

"Nothing but a heat burn," I said. "Let's see if anyone knows how to extricate this knight out of his can, then get out of here."

I started to turn, then almost slapped myself in the face. "Wait a minute," I said to Squid. "There's something else we need to do first. Ward—come on—we've got to find that merc we knocked down."

After a few minutes of searching, we found the Unity guy sprawling limply on the ground. We found him laying on his side in the bushes. He looked pretty wrecked. I waved my hand in front of his visor but he didn't respond, so I decided to unlatch his helmet.

"Wait, don't touch him!" Ward warned me. "I've heard these guys can hack you ten ways from Sunday. He gets inside your suit AI and next thing you know your emergency bandage foam is getting poured down your throat or something."

"We hit him with enough electromagnetism to burn out a power station," I reminded him. "I'm gonna risk it." I reached down and fumbled with the guy's helmet and took it off.

Beneath the helmet, the guy's face was masked by some sort of a black shroud. I carefully pulled it off, revealing one of the ugliest faces I've ever seen in my life. The guy's head was half silvery metal and black plastic, and both his eyes looked like silvery laboratory gemstones, backlit and multi-faceted. I looked a little closer and saw tiny fibrous wires connecting man and machine, as well as clusters of subdermal chips that raised small bumps on his slug-white skin, as if he'd developed a strangely geometric case of the hives.

"Damn," Ward said. "That guy ain't right."

Suddenly, the man took a hissing intake of breath. "Identify yourselves," he said.

"All those facets and you can't see us?" Ward replied.

"Our optical functionality is compromised," he said weakly.

"That may be," I said. "You're going to tell us why you're here, machine-head."

"We will tell you nothing," he said, raising a hand dismissively.

"We need some answers," Ward said. "You're coming with us."

"We will tell you nothing!"

The man took a convulsive breath, then lay perfectly still.

"I think he's dead," I said, after watching him for a moment.

"The EMP probably cooked his circuits," Ward said.

"At least we can haul in his corpse and take him apart," I muttered, replacing the guy's facial shroud and helmet, then hoisting him over my shoulder. I saw the militia was already extricating the surviving knight from his war chassis. "Let's get out of here."

Chapter 9

"Their attacks just aren't making sense," I said, looking over a map Ward had projected on the wall in the mess room. "They're taking territory in pieces here and there, then hitting a little factory or something, killing a few guys, then moving back out. I'm not seeing any sort of coherent offensive."

I'd successfully pawned off my officer screening assignment to Squid, since Captain Yost agreed it was more important for us to figure out exactly what the Axiosi and their cyborg buddies were up to. After several days of research and analysis with little to show for it, I'd gathered some of the guys together to have a few drinks and throw a few ideas around.

I pointed at a large fuel refinery. "They could have hit that, but they went around and blew up a small college instead. Over here," I said, pointing at a section of green, "there's a huge buried cable line that provides a lot of power to the capital, coming from the geothermal station up north. They marched over it, bypassing the transformer station here, then trashed a manufacturer of foil display screen tech."

"Those are used for mobile surveillance centers," Ward said. "Isn't that what we used when we tracked that butterfly priest that Vero blasted to death?"

"Not quite the same thing. Those you can crinkle up and then un-crinkle and stick to a wall. These are made to be permanent fixtures. It's the kind of overlay that goes inside a windscreen display. A laminate layer with embedded image projection."

"So it's just a commercial outfit?" Jones asked.

"Yeah," I replied. "They supply a lot of civilian automobile and hovercraft, some space transports. Minor military contracts for the tech, but something like 95 percent consumer sales, when I looked up the numbers."

"Not worth hitting compared to a refinery," Ward said, finishing a swig of beer and popping another top. Pitt had commandeered a few dozen twelve-packs from somewhere and quietly installed them in the motel's commercial fridge, much to the chagrin of the staff. "They could have hit that cable, too."

"Right. And if you look here," I zoomed in and pointed to a red X on top of a cluster of buildings, "you'll see a zero-friction bearing company was nailed. It's not even a manufacturer, just an importer of parts manufactured in the Kantillon asteroid belt. They're used in cranes and other industrial high-stress joints. Another hit was here," I pointed to another red X. "A superconductor facility. They also bombed a little government archive up here," I said, pointing to yet another strike. "They're not even holding the territory. They come in, hit the target, then retreat to a fortified position."

"What the hell," Jones said. "It's almost like they're just nailing things at random." He'd rejoined us after a local doc put him in the de-concusser or whatever that big tube thing is where they work on your head. He didn't seem to make any less sense than usual, as far as I could tell.

"Maybe they're just trying to lure the knights into ambushes," Edgerton said.

"At first, maybe, but obviously it hasn't been working since we figured out how they were taking them down and talked some sense into them."

"Maybe they're targeting the knights in some other way," Ward said. "It has to be about the knights somehow."

"What, the knights like to take continuing education courses at night and do construction on the weekend?" Jones said. He sounded skeptical, and not without reason.

"Damned if I know," Ward said. "But I'll bet there's a link between these hits and the knights. They're Sfodria's main defense. The militia is worse than useless, and if I were gonna knock this place down, I'd take out the 500 knights. Once they're out of the picture, they can roll up the militia, no problem."

"Of course!" I said as the pieces snapped together in my head. "I saw all the random crap getting hit, then looked up the numbers on these places and saw they were civilian. But that's just the report to the public, right? All the tech on the knight's suits is classified. They're cutting edge."

"Maybe they use those crane bearings in their joints," Zelag said.

"Right, and maybe foil display in their helmets," Ward added. "Superconductors for computational power, who knows."

"What about the archive and the college?"

"Babbage has an idea on those," Edgerton said. "The former contained a massive amount of encrypted archives. Some of those might have been important to the design of the knights' robotic battlesuits."

"And the college?" I asked, grabbing my first beer of the evening and popping the top.

"They had a robotics lab. Best in the nation," Edgerton said.

"Maybe there were researchers there that worked on the suits," Jones said. "Or a secret lab or something."

"Now we're getting somewhere," I said, then pointed at another red X. "But what about the dog park up here?"

"What?" came multiple voices.

"Never mind. Just screwing with you."

I stayed up past midnight looking for possible connections between the knights and the strange pattern of destruction laid out on the map. The problem was that if you look hard enough, you can find false patterns almost anywhere. Hell, if they actually had bombed a dog park, I could have theorized it was because the maid of a top armor specialist walked his prize poodle there and the loss of the dog would demoralize the guy and hurt the war effort. But I wanted to focus on credible connections that would help me understand and anticipate the enemy actions, and since the mech development was completely classified, I had to guess as best as I could and rule out big stretches. I managed to link about three-quarters of the pattern to something that could be reasonably related to suit development, research or supply for the knights.

I decided to take what I'd pieced together to the Lord General. He would know more about the manufacturing infrastructure, so I could let him run with it. He was arrogant, but he wasn't stupid, and now that he understood his knights were being targeted on the field, there was a good chance that he'd buy the Axiosi were striking at them in more surreptitious ways.

I listed the attacks with their locations, summarized my conclusions, and put a data chip together. Then I sent a message to Captain Yost asking for another audience with the Lord General.

The next day Yost and I stood in the chamber of audience again across from the Lord General. This time, only a pair of knights were present, neither of whom I recognized. Neither of them was my red-and-brown battle buddy.

"You have something useful for us?" the Lord General asked as soon as we entered, not bothering with any introductions.

"I hope so, Lord General," I replied, then held up my data chip. "Do you have a projector?"

He snapped his fingers and a young man in a white robe entered from a previously hidden door and took the chip from me, handing me a small remote in return. A couple of moments later, a projection of my report appeared in the center of the room.

"As you can see," I pointed at the projection, "there is what appears to be a strategic purpose behind the enemy attacks."

"Our analysis indicates that it is random," the Lord General said. "It's little more than raiding meant to demoralize the populace. The Axiosi have always tried to stir up the commoners, to no avail."

I turned to the two knights. "Noble sirs, have the members of your knightly order had any difficulties obtaining anything you need for your armor recently?"

"That is classified information," the Lord General objected.

I was surprised when one of the knights waved his hand dismissively at the general. "Never mind that, Landros. This is the hireling who stood over Sir Enright when he was disabled on the field. He knows we are not invulnerable."

Interesting. It seemed the aristocratic order was a little more egalitarian than one would have thought.

"There have been multiple issues with the supply chain, though nothing beyond minor annoyances yet yet. My own mecha is currently suffering from an issue in the wiring harness, but it remains fully operational. The shipment of parts we'd ordered from Rhysalan was shelled inside the hangar. None of this information must leave this chamber. If any of the commoners knew we had a hint of vulnerability in any sense, it would lead to panic."

"I'm sure," I agreed. Or rebellion, which is what I suspected the Axiosi intended. "What I have concluded in looking at the pattern of attacks is that what at first appears random is actually a slowly closing net tightening around you and your noble order. Bit by bit, step by step, they are knocking out your structural supports. There have even been some murders of men I concluded are your engineers."

"Yes," the knight mused. "We lost at least a dozen experienced mechanics over the last two months. It had not occurred to us that they were anything beyond than the regular losses to be expected in Ares's playground."

"You know better than me how many of these targets can be confirmed to be related to the supply and keeping of your order. I will leave the data with you."

"Well," the Lord General said after a silence. "It seems you may have learned something useful to us after all."

"Yes, Lord General," Captain Yost said. "Although you may recall that Corporal Falkland's hypothesis concerning nanotech-based weapons was correct."

"I need recall no such thing," the Lord General said. "We have not finished the analysis of Sir Enright's armor."

"Come now, Landros, there is no reason to delay the obvious," the knight who had spoken up earlier said. I wondered if he might be a rival for the Lord General's position. "There's a time for honor and there's a time to face up to the facts. Sir Enright's death was not natural."

"His death?" I blurted, taken by surprise.

"Yes," the knight answered calmly. "His augment overloaded his brain as a result of the disruption the nanite attack caused his mech. His body was unharmed, but all higher functions were lost."

"We need to protect the remaining knights," Yost said. "Tommy's report has me convinced—you guys are in a net, as he said. That net closes, you may very well lose this war."

"The knights have lasted for a thousand years," the second knight said. "We will last a thousand more."

"I hope that's the case," I said. "You kick ass and everyone recognizes that. You're freaking 20-foot tall metal monsters with laser swords. But the bad guys have found your Achilles heel now, and they're hitting you on the field and they're taking away your supply lines and killing the little people that keep you running. You've already lost an unprecedented number of your order."

"So what would you have us do, corporal?" the Lord General said. "We will not leave the field of battle in the hands of commoners."

"With that in mind—if you are convinced you must keep fielding the knights—then they will need escorts," I replied, flipping to my suggestions list at the end of the report. I'd sketched out a digital picture of a knight accompanied by an entourage of little guys with rifles. It was all stick figures, but it made the point. "Put some guys with EMP rifles around them and have them hit the enemy first, plus don't let anyone close enough to launch a nano attack. The knight should be viewed as a mobile artillery platform, with an infantry screen. As far as we can tell, the enemy's nano-weapons have an effective range of about 100 meters. Maybe their projectiles don't fly well or maybe there is some sort of com connection required. I don't know, but it's clear that leaving your heavies exposed isn't viable anymore."

The Lord General snorted. "Let me guess. Now this is where you pitch your services. 24 mercenaries in pretty white armor supporting each and every knight at some ungodly sum per day, am I right?"

"No, Lord General," I said. "I suggest you utilize your own militia. Buy a few crates of L-24 fusion assisted EMP rifles, we'll train them up in platoons, after which they'll go out with the knights and keep the enemy nanites from neutralizing them.

"Impossible," the first knight said. "The militia cannot keep up with us. And to hide behind the commoners, to permit them to serve as our shields, that would be dishonorable!"

"We'd probably step on them," the second knight said. "It might even be accidental. You soldiers-for-hire cannot be expected to understand, but for us, the highest honor is for a knight to take the field with the burden of the state's defense resting upon his shoulders. This is not a concern of commoners nor is it their duty. We are the incarnate shield of state—we fight so they may live! What you propose is the reverse of that."

"I understand these combined arms tactics would be new to you," I said. "But you're putting yourselves into a damned stupid position–"

"That is enough," the Lord General interrupted loftily. "We thank you for your report, Corporal Falkland. The data will be analyzed. We will be in touch if we require more from you. You are dismissed."

I stalked out of the chamber with Yost, still limping a little on my burned leg, and fuming at the knights' complete lack of strategic sense. They might as well throw themselves naked at machine gun nests armed with nothing but primitive metal swords.

"Damned stupid?" Yost said after the doors slammed shut behind us.

"Yeah," I said. "Sorry about that. I got a little carried away."

"No skin off my nose," he said. "That outburst would have gotten you fired from the sales department, but the fact is, you're right on this one. Their tactics need tweaking at the very least, and maybe it's better to keep the knights off the field altogether, but these guys are so caught up in their honor that they don't realize the battlefield has moved beyond them. The Theodosian walls stood for a thousand years. Then some stupid damned Kraut made a cannon for the Sultan and their utility ended practically overnight."

"I have no idea what you're talking about," I said truthfully.

"Never mind," he said. "You did fine. Just watch your mouth next time."

We headed back to base in a borrowed Toymo jeep, winding down the long road from the huge plateau where the hall was situated and down through the city beneath. I drove in silence, thinking through our futile audience with the Lord General.

So, that knight in red and brown had died on the field—that I did not expect. For all his haughtiness, I have to admit I kind of liked the guy. And he obviously had picked me out to taunt, so maybe he felt the same in his weird aristocratic way. We might have been friends at some point. At the very least, I felt like he was an ally. When someone saves your ass in battle, then you save theirs, it changes everything. I don't care if the biggest SOB in the world is in the trench next to me. When shit gets real, you watch each other's backs. Then sometimes you find that you not only can tolerate the SOB, you love him like a brother. Or some crap like that.

But thinking about Sir Enright, I had a pretty good idea what had happened and how he must have died. The nanites had begun burrowing through his armor once the projectile struck. First they wrecked the suit's sensors, then its servo-mechanicals, and then its digital systems. Only when the mech was entirely disabled did they turn their attention to the man inside it. I'm not an expert on the tech side of things, but I knew this was a bad business. And it occurred to me that this might just be some early beta testing of the nanite weapon. What if instead of shutting everything down, the Unity could grab control of a mech's systems live on the field and turn them into a remote weapon to use against their own side? I imagined one of the robotic monsters turning on my squad. Even Wardogs wouldn't stand a chance.

I found myself wondering if we could get approval for micro-nuclear ammunition.

"Yost," the captain suddenly spoke out loud, taking a call. "What? I see. No, no idea on our end. Just spoke with the Lord General. Yeah, good idea. No. I can't spare you. Right. Keep trying."

The call ended and we continued to drive on in silence. I suppressed the urge to ask him what had happened. Yost chewed on his thumbnail and looked out at the scattered lights across the desert, obviously contemplating something.

"Falkland," he said at long last.

"Yes sir," I said.

"That was Pitt. He's got a bit of an inside track with a local official who told him something just went down back at the capital tonight."

"We were just there," I said. "I didn't notice anything. What's the deal?"

Yost shrugged. "The guy said he wouldn't talk except in person. Pitt's guess is that their coms are compromised somehow. Pitt wants to go see, but we can't risk our logistics at this point, so I'm sending you back to assess the situation."

"Yessir," I said. I was tempted to say something sarcastic about being more expendable than Pitt, except the captain was right. If everything was going to hell in a hurry, then the whole unit's survival might well come down to his ability to get us the stuff we needed.

We pulled in to base as he finished his sentence. I could hear the shouts and hits of a pick-up slingball game taking place on the other side of the hangar. Some of the shouts were in the local dialect so I was guessing some of our guys had roped in some of their militia trainees.

"Take someone smart with you, Falkland, but don't take your whole team," Yost said. "I would suggest Ward. The others should keep working with the militia, and start training them on that screen tactic for the knights. You get to Pitt's guy and see if he'll spill his guts in person. We'll get you an aircab, it'll be faster. Pitt will send the location to your system."

"Copy that, Captain!" I hopped out of the vehicle and threw him a salute he didn't bother to return as he sped off towards the building that served as his command post.

I walked through the hangar just in time to see Zelag sling a strike past a hulking militia member. "Not fair at all," one of the militia guys argued, shaking his head. "He's got a robot arm. It's like boxing with a robot!"

Zelag nodded. "If my machine-assisted superiority is more than you can handle, one of my brothers-in-arms must take my place," he offered piously, holding out his glove to Jones.

"Not so fast," Jones said, shirtless and glistening with sweat beneath the lights. He put his hand on Zelag's shoulder. "There is discrimination taking place, based on this man's infirmity."

The more the militia jeered and laughed, the more sanctimonious his voice became. "My brothers, let he who casts judgment, first consider if that judgment might also fall upon themselves. Consider my superbly muscled buttocks, for example."

I didn't wait for the punchline. Ward wasn't there. If it had been left up to me, I would have taken Zelag, but I had my orders.

I found Ward beating the living daylights out of a punching bag in the gym we'd rigged up.

"Ward, we have to go to the capital," I said.

"What?" he replied, tapping the side of his head to turn down the music he must have been listening to. "When?"

"You and I are going to the capital. Now. Something's going down and the captain doesn't like it. We have to talk to Pitt first, though."

He nodded, stopped the bag from swinging, then swung around and sucker punched it one more time before picking up his bag and heading to our quarters.

"Where's Pitt?" I asked, grabbing a passing logistics flunky in the hall.

"Down at the end, sir," the kid said, pointing to the storeroom at the end of the hall.

Pitt was poring over a complicated series of spreadsheets on a screen when we poked our heads into the room. He didn't even look up when I knocked on the open door to announce our presence.

"Mm hmm," he said.

"Pitt, it's Falkland and Ward. What's up at the capital?"

He tapped a few times on the screen, grunted in dissatisfaction, and spun around. "Hey Tommy. Hey Jack. What can I do for you guys?"

"We got tagged to go check out your guy. What's the lowdown?"

"All right. So, Potchi is this asset I've cultivated in the city. He's a low-level distribution guy, but his connections up and down the supply chain are pretty good. He called and told me something bad was going on but he wouldn't talk about it. He sounded upset, though."

"Captain said you thought the coms were compromised."

"Yeah, the way he said he couldn't talk made me think someone was listening in, maybe on the line, maybe in person."

"You think you know this guy well enough to take it seriously?"

"He's not the panicking type. He's a merchant. Cold-blooded. Sell his grandmother if you offered the right price. But he's a numbers guy, not some sort of drama queen prone to hyperbole. He made it sound like the sky was falling. Trust me, otherwise I wouldn't have called Yost at all. It was totally out of character, so I thought maybe we'd better check it out."

Ward and I looked at each other. Ward shrugged.

"Pretty thin," he said.

"We got our orders," I pointed out. He shrugged again. "All right, thanks, Pitt," I said, but the logistics officer was already back at his screen again, wrestling with his numbers.

Pitt's asset lived in a modest home at the edge of a huge field of some sort of green-tipped grain. Next door was a much larger house surrounded by high walls. We approached the estate from the air and I noticed the cab didn't pass over the edge of the field before we landed at Potchi's place, though it would have been faster. The vehicle was driverless so I mentioned it to Ward as we touched down.

"Might be some sort of airspace laws," he said. "I'll bet that's a knight's residence. Maybe this guy is some sort of squire who lives close to his boss."

"Makes sense," I said as we stepped out into the cool evening air. A child's scooter lay alongside the driveway and a neat garden with a stone image of a saint or a god or something was just outside the front door. Outside the edge of the green yard was the same dead scrub we'd seen on the rest of this campaign. The estate behind the house was much the same, green fields bordered by arid ground. My guess was that one of the perks of working for the knights was a little extra water for the yard. Before we reached the door, the lights came on over the porch and a kid came outside and saw us in our battle suits. His eyes widened and he tore back in through the front door. A moment later, a middle-aged guy came out.

"Wardogs?" he said, peering at us. "Is one of you Pitt?"

"No sir," I replied. "We came at his request. Can you provide us the information you were unable to provide him earlier?"

The guy looked around at the road and at our taxi, satisfying himself that no one else was present. He nodded. "Come on in," he said. "Please excuse the disarray."

We stepped inside and I entirely failed to notice anything out of order, let alone in disarray. Everything was neat and tidy, austere in its simplicity, except for the occasional child's toy. The boy watched us walk in and I waved to him. I heard him say "sojers" in an awed tone as he stared at our armor. At least someone was awed.

"We'll talk in my office," Potchi said. "Donalla, I have visitors, would you mind watching Morrelos?"

A woman with grief-reddened eyes and unkempt hair stepped into the room, bowed to us, then went to where the kid sat. We followed Potchi to his office and he carefully shut the door, then adjusted something inside an alcove to the side of the door. "So we can't be heard," he said, then turned to us. "Do you always wear your suits?" he said.

"Most of the time," I replied. "We're interchangeable units, presenting a single face to the world or something like that."

"I see," he said, sitting down. "Please, sit."

Ward and I demurred, not wanting to shatter his furniture with the weight of our armor.

Potchi took a breath. "I called Pitt because there has been a murder. Several murders."

"Murders?" I said. "Why did you call us, then?"

"Because the men murdered were knights of the Blood."

"More than one knight was murdered? How many? When did this happen."

"Just today. Five were killed. They were murdered in their homes," he said, shaking his head. "No, I take that back. Four of them died in their homes. One died in his skycar."

"Does anyone know this yet?" I said.

"Not about all five," he said. "I have been in contact with other squires as the evening has progressed. We have our own communication network."

"But you couldn't simply tell the knights?" I said.

"No," he said. "Because of the way they died. I didn't know what I could do, or to whom I could turn. Then I thought of Pitt and your organization."

"Back up," Ward said. "We've got shielded communications. Hell, the average consumer line is hard for anything short of a military AI to hack, and I'm sure you've got better encryption than that if you're working right with the Stratocracy's leaders on a daily basis. You think whoever is doing this can listen?"

"Yes," he said. "Because that's how they're killing them."

"The knights?" I asked. "They're killing them through their communication system?"

"The first one victim was apparently Sir Hiktessi. While his manservant was trimming his beard, the sonic razor overloaded and tore half the knight's face off, destroying his brain. Before committing suicide, the manservant called Sir Hiktessi's squire and told him what happened. The servant blamed himself, though the safety features on a sonic shouldn't have let the poor commoner kill someone with the thing unless he perhaps pounded it into a man's head with a hammer. Squire Kollomi informed the council of knights of the death, then of course conferred with the Circle of Squires over our private net. Even as we mourned, another report came in that Sir Polyporus' skycar had been lost in the Makkens, and then, just after that, Sir Waldreno was found face-down on the steps of the library. His cochlear implant was smoking when they found him. Even as we started to realize something horrible was taking place, there was another death."

The man stopped and took a deep breath, folding his hands in his lap. To my surprise, I noted a tear rolling down his face.

"Spill it," Ward said, having no time for the man's grief.

"My master was the fourth victim," he said after a moment. "I called his private line after the third death. He picked up and acknowledged my concern but told me not to be overly worried. He was a great man. A true warrior."

"And?" I said.

"And while we were talking, I heard a strange sound that crept into the line. Almost like static. But that was unusual, since the line runs directly between my house and his, so the connection is always crystal clear. It's shielded and quite secure, so I assumed it was a wiring problem or something, but as Sir Warris spoke, his voice just vanished into the static. I closed the line and called again but got nothing, so I punched in the codes that let me into his field and simply ran straight to his house. When I got there, he was standing on the porch, hands on the back of a therapeutic chair he sometimes uses to strengthen his spine after a day in the field. 'Sir Warris,' I said, but he said nothing. So I stepped closer, then I saw his eyes were open—he was staring off into the distance. I dared to finally put my hand on his arm and I received an electric shock that almost threw me to the ground Then he just fell to the ground himself... dead."

"The chair killed him?" Ward said.

"Yes, it must have been the chair. But the line died first, which made me wonder if they were listening to it, if they could hear us. You know, they say the Unity are here on the planet. Their machines can get into computers, so perhaps they could do this, they could kill the knights with their demon technology!"

"It's possible," I said. "And we know they're targeting the mech pilots."

"How long has it been since you checked in with the other squires?" Ward asked.

"Two hours," Potchi admitted. "I called in after the death of my master and only came back here to the house to put my things in order before I join him."

"Join him?" I said.

"I will open my veins," Potchi said proudly. "It is my obligation as his squire to accompany him to the next life."

"Damn, man," Ward said. "You sure you don't want to just look for another job or something? You have a wife and a kid to look after!"

The man shook his head. "Absolutely not. My son will grow up knowing that his father did his duty!"

"Suit yourself," I said. "But before you kick off, will you check that screen again. Maybe there's more news."

The man nodded, flipped off something in the alcove, then logged in on a small console. After a moment, he gasped. "May the Gods have mercy!"

"What?" Ward asked.

"Four knights are dead!"

"When?" I asked.

"The last one took place an hour ago. Sir Forogloss."

"How?" Ward said.

"He died in his shower," Potchi said, his eyes scanning over the messages. "Another died while tending his greenhouse. Another fell dead in the People's archive while doing research at a workstation. O gods, how have we failed you?" he cried, clutching his head in his hands. "Oh gods, why do you judge us so harshly?"

"I think we know what we need to know," I said to Ward. "Thank you, sir."

The man nodded, then grabbed my armored arm tightly. "Do not let them win, I beg you. Avenge our deaths!"

"We intend to kill them," I said. *So long as we keep getting paid, anyhow*, I thought but didn't think he needed to hear that. "And we're very good at that."

We walked out, past the kid and the man's wife. Ward ruffled the kid's hair as he passed. "Be tough, kid," he said.

We climbed back into our taxi and it took us back to base. After we were in the air I wondered if the Unity might have control of the autopilot. Visions of us hurling to the ground flashed through my head but I pushed them out. I didn't call in, though, in case the squire was right. Maybe they would hear my call and take out the taxi, who knows? I was with the local guy on calling. Better safe than sorry.

We made it back safely and Ward and I hunted down the captain to give him the sitrep before we turned in. It was after zero two quarter but he was sitting with Pitt in the cafeteria, nursing a mug of coffee.

"Any reason you didn't call in?" Yost said.

"Pitt's asset thinks communications may be compromised," I replied. "Things are bad. Eight deaths, all weird accidents."

"Which aren't accidents," Ward said.

"Not accidents?" Yost said. "Who is dead?"

"Knights," I replied. "Eight knights are dead under bizarre circumstances. Crashed skycars, malfunctioning furniture and razors, crazy stuff."

"Unity hacking," Yost said. "Targeted kills."

"Exactly," I said. "No way it was anything else. Also, Pitt, you lost your asset."

"Dammit, Tommy!" He slammed his fist on the table. "What did you do? Interrogate him?"

"No, we behaved ourselves. It's just that he's a squire to one of the dead knights, so he's got to off himself. It's a matter of honor or something."

"You're kidding!" Pitt shook his head. "Ah, well, that's a damn shame."

"Yeah, especially for the wife and kid," muttered Ward.

The captain was completely uninterested in the local customs. "First, they were knocking out the supply chain, now they're going for the knights directly. The Lord General is in over his head. The Sfodrians simply aren't equipped to deal with this."

"Neither are we," Ward said. "They're hacking into secure lines running directly between two residences. This isn't like a public web hack. One knight was apparently murdered through the overload of his cochlear implant. We have to assume that everything we're doing can be monitored, and everything we've got can be hacked."

"Including our suits," I pointed out.

"Acknowledged," Yost said. "All right, I have to take this to the Lord General right now. You good to go, Falkland?"

"Now?" Ward said.

I dialed up a stim and closed my eyes as the pick-me-up coursed through my blood. "Good to go, sir!"

We drove back up to the Hall of Meeting and found the Lord General already there, along with ten of his knights. They seemed surprised to see us, but allowed us to talk.

"So?" Lord General Landros asked Yost. "You have heard of the murders?"

"Yes," he replied. "Corporal Falkland has been to the capital and spoke directly with the squire of the late Sir Warris. We are confident that this is the work of the mercenaries from the Unity."

"We concur," the Lord General said. "It would appear your original analysis was correct, Corporal," he said, nodding at me. That was all the apology I was going to get, I could see. "Cowards! To kill a man in his sleep, or in the shower! They have no honor."

"Of course they don't have honor," Yost said. "They don't even know what it is. They're not human."

"All the knights must be protected, whether they wish it or not," the Lord General declared. "But how shall we accomplish that, when these honorless monsters can even reach into the fortified homes of their noble ancestors?"

"They must all disconnect," I told him. "From everything. Get them totally offline and keep them away from all electrics, all nets, all digitals. Even their medical implants need to be removed. Nothing is safe!"

"We cannot take such extreme measures," a knight said angrily. "We would render ourselves infants, helpless and vulnerable."

"We are helpless and vulnerable now," a second knight pointed out, more sensibly, in my opinion.

"Our noble ancestors relied on naught but simple weapons and the might of their arms," another knight said. "It won't kill us to go back in time. It will kill us if we don't, however. I have already had my cerebral port completely deactivated by my house physician. I suggest the rest of you do the same."

I thought of the jack in my own head. WDI tech was robust, by human standards, but I doubted it would withstand a concentrated attack by the half-machine posthumans.

"Let it be done, at once," said the Lord General. "Every knight is to consider it a battle order in the service of the State. He turned to Yost. "Is there anything you can do to stop these monstrous cowards?"

"Yes," Yost said. "We're going to kill them."

Chapter 10

Killing embedded transhumans is easier said than done. Sure, you can nail them with a focused EMP pulse if you're close enough, but what about the guys that are sitting in some shielded bunker somewhere, burrowing through the 'net right into some poor bastard's neural interface? Finding those guys wasn't going to be easy, and we knew that once they considered us to be a threat, they would certainly come after us.

"So how do we hunt cyborgs?" I asked, after the captain gave me the go-ahead to start the brainstorm session. "Any ideas, throw them out. I don't care how stupid they might seem."

I'd been able to pull ten guys together for a quick hashing out of our situation. Squid, Ace, Jock, Edgerton, Pitt, Jones, Park, Ward, Zelag, and Captain Yost. The captain only had half a kilosec free, so we were hoping to nail down a plan in that time period.

"Metal detectors," Park suggested.

"Did you see the dead one?" Squid said, blowing smoke across the metal folding table towards Park. "He had metal in him, sure, but I'll bet that doesn't show up any more than a grunt in armor, hauling a rifle."

"Infrared," Park said, then took a delicate sip of herbal tea he'd gotten from who knows where. "They probably have a different heat signature than a real guy."

"Probably," I said. "But we don't know."

"Not much range on infrared sensors," Zelag commented.

"We need a live one to study," Ward said. "We killed the last one. And the one before that suicided. I think the real problem is that they'll all suicide rather than talk."

"We get anything useful from the corpse?" Jones asked.

"No," Pitt said. "The lab guys said he was toasted inside. Not much more than half-melted wires running through jerky. Amazing he was still twitching when you boys found him." Pitt shrugged and swigged some coffee. "Too bad, too, because I've got a console that keeps acting up and I could use a good IT professional."

We looked at him blankly and he ducked his head a little. "Just a joke. Carry on."

"Maybe we could combine infrared and metal detection," Ace mused. "Our eyes could tell the difference if one of these guys wasn't in a suit. Why not tweak some sensors so they're looking for the little things? The distribution of metal in one of these guys might be a little different than in a regular soldier, plus we could maybe look for a little difference in temps. Maybe they run a little fever compared to an unmodified man. Or maybe they don't, maybe they're cold-blooded or something. We should have the lab guys here, really."

"That's true," I said. "My fault. We should have got some techs in here."

"Sharks," Edgerton said.

We all turned to look at him. "What the hell?" Jones said.

"Sharks," Edgerton said. "Everyone knows they have a sixth sense. They can find their prey even in pitch black conditions."

"Isn't that just their sense of smell?" Ward asked. "They say they can smell just a drop of blood from a hundred kilometers away."

"No, of course not," Edgerton said. "It's electromagnetic. Every guy around this table has his own electrical field. Even bugs have their own electrical field. I think I could modify a standard sensor to detect their electromagnetospheres."

"How is that different from what a metal detector would see?" I asked him.

"Metal is detected by magnetic fields, but it's not the same. Everything is glowing with electric energy, at least on a low level. There are always lots of little discharges inside your body taking place."

"What kind of range?" Zelag asked.

"Considering how much bigger their electromagnetic fields must be, they'd light up like a Christmas tree. I'd guess we're talking kilometers."

"That's good," I said. "That's real good!"

"This force shield business sounds like voodoo," Jones objected.

"Platypi," Zelag countered.

"What the hell is a platter pie, Cyborg?" Squid said.

"Something that looks funnier than you do, Squid," Zelag said. "They're an old Earth animal. Still some of them scattered here and there on the colonies, thanks to the re-seeders. They're a strange little animal with webbed feet, fur and a bill like a duck, but they're a mammal, I think."

"Great," Jones said. "What's up with the zoology lesson?"

"That's just it. They can sense magnetic fields with their bills," Zelag pressed on. "Like Edgerton said about sharks."

"Exactly," Edgerton said.

"Wonderful," Jones said. "So, we just need a big crate of platypuses or something?"

"Can these platter pussies be taught to shoot Feempers?" Ace said.

"Enough, boys!" Captain Yost shut them up. "Let's get back on track. Falkland, continue."

"Thanks," I said. "Forget the platypus, men. We don't care about whatever the hell they are. But we do care about finding these Unity mercs and if there's some way of seeing their energy field or something we can use, great. Edgerton and Zelag, you talk to the techs about it."

"We should mount the sensors on our aerial drones," Ace said.

"Obviously," I said. "More importantly, we'll want to get the sensors to the knights as soon as we know they work. If the knights cut their coms and stay high, they can act as both scouts and artillery."

"Big-ass drones, basically," Ward remarked.

"This sounds promising," the captain declared said. "I need to get back to work, but let me know whatever you boys need and Pitt will get it for you. Edgerton, you're point on this. Drop whatever else you're doing and get this electro-whatever sensor working!"

"Big-ass scout drones with rockets and plasma cannons," Jones said dreamily.

"Off the chain!" Park said.

"Check it out, Falkland," Edgerton said, pointing to a drone with a duct-taped sensor assembly on the front. "Shark sensors."

"Shiny," I said, not really knowing what I was looking at. Sergeant Edgerton caressed the drone with his fingers. "It can correctly ID bioelectric fields at a kilometer away. Here, check this out."

He made a couple of adjustments to the drone and the drone started humming. It was one of those rounded, lightly armored super-light surveillance jobs that run on antigrav. They're cheap as dirt and you can launch them all day over enemy positions without caring if they get shot down. They're about the size of a big bird, but with more wingspan.

"Now it's scanning," Edgerton said. "Here, look at my tablet." He handed me a small display and I watched as the room was resolved into gray and white. "That's you and me," he said, pointing to a tall softly glowing figure next to a thinner and slightly shorter one one.

"What's up with my head?" I asked, looking at the screen.

"Where it's glowing white?" Edgerton said. "Probably a jack. You have a brainjack, right?"

"Yeah," I said, looking closer. "And my elbow—there's a darker spot there. Wait—that's gotta be shrapnel, maybe?"

"Right," Edgerton said. "It's not radiating like the rest of your cells."

"Nice," I said.

"We could see the wires and all that stuff running through the cyborgs," Edgerton said. "Cool, huh?"

"Yeah," I said. "This is cool."

"I've dubbed it the Sharknose model 1A," Edgerton said.

"Great work, Sarge," I said sincerely. "Now let's see how it works in the field!"

"Platterpussy away!" Jones said as our drone took to the air.

He, Ward, Zelag and I were out near a known Axiosi position, hoping to spot ourselves a Unity merc. Edgerton, Park, Jock and Morrel were on another patrol forty kilometers north of our position, doing the same thing. We'd hauled our drone with us in a pack, disassembled for easy carrying. They can be broken down into three parts for portability and they weigh almost nothing. If we saw an enemy patrol with the drone's cameras, we'd send it closer and flip on the electromagnetic thing and see if anything that looked like a cyborg appeared on the sensors. If it didn't, we'd just dodge the patrol and keep hunting; we weren't interested in the enemy regulars.

We'd hiked for an hour through some scrubby woods after being dropped off until we hit a good clear space of rocky ground. It was early morning and the sun was just coming up in the purple sky above. Man, my eyes were really starting to get tired of purple.

"Get it more altitude," I said to Ward as he drove the drone higher.

"It's getting up there," he said, monitoring the craft's climbing spiral on the warm air rising from the ground. The antigrav on these drones wasn't all that powerful. It was more like floating a helium balloon than the kind of elevator thrust you got from a serious antigrav engine. The drones weren't fast but they could stay in the air for days without draining their batteries. They rarely lasted all that long, though, as the enemy made a habit of using them for target practice.

"Okay, we're up," Ward said, putting the drone's small control interface back in its rucksack. I could just see the drone up above, a small dark speck in the purple sky. "It's on a standard search pattern grid now. We can just watch and wait. The AI will let us know when it spots anything that isn't us."

"Let's get back in the shade," Jones said. "I'm ready for breakfast."

We found a shadier spot and squeezed protein paste and artificial cheese into our mouths while we waited for our drone to spot

something.   I wondered what Sfodrian girls were like.   I hadn't
seen a single one in the militia or support teams.   That squire guy's
wife wasn't bad at all.   Maybe they kept them in cages or something. Or maybe they were so hot they didn't trust the men around
them.   Yeah, that was probably the case. All of them 5'7" with
blonde hair and pierced bellybuttons, pressing grapes with their long
legs and bare feet, just waiting for a mercenary with a heart of
gold to sweep them off into space for a life of adventure and lots
of–"

"Got something," Ward said, interrupting my thoughts. "Looks
like a small patrol, five klicks to the west. They were holed up under
the trees, got some anti-scanner tech—still surprised we hadn't seen
them yet. Still blurry as hell on the camera." He fished out the drone
controls and took back manual control.

"Can the platterpussy see them?" I asked.

"I've switched it on but we're not close enough for the new scanner."

"Maybe take it low, then fly over their position so they don't have
time to shoot it down?"

"Yep," Ward said, watching the data and visuals on his tablet. "You
guys can watch the scan while I'm flying her if you want to link the
second tablet in the sack."

Jones pulled it out and took the electronic scanner feed. We saw a
bunch of rippling gray and then a lighter patch started to resolve in
one corner.

"Coming in," Ward said. The image zoomed, and the lighter patch
turned into glowing blobs. "We'll just gather data on this sweep, so
you might not see much live. The tablet can tighten up what we're
seeing after we pull her back." The glowing images moved across the
screen, then were gone.

"All right," Ward said, "I'm sending her back up out of range. They
definitely saw her and I don't want to risk losing her."

"Well," Jones said. "Those blobs look like cyborgs to you?"

"Nope," I said.

"Just wait," Ward said, setting down the drone controls and picking up his tablet. "Okay, we got an image. We just need to enhance it. Okay, there, have a look at that."

Now we saw the shapes of three guys. Their armor was dark but their bodies glowed a pale gray around it against the darker background of the ground. All three of them had bright halos around their heads.

"What's up with the glowing heads?" Jones asked.

"Helmets," Ward said. "It's probably the active electronic in their heads-up displays."

"I see some glowing lines here and there on their bodies, too," Zelag said.

"Probably suit sensors," Ward said. "I'll see if we can look through the armor better."

He made some adjustments and the armor mostly faded away, leaving just the shape of men, though still with halos. The bright lines showed up brighter and the rifle batteries were glowing now.

"I don't see anything here that can't be explained by normal suits and weapons," Ward said.

"So they're just regular humans?" Zelag asked.

"Yeah, I'd say so," Ward said.

"Good, we got ourselves a baseline," I said. "Later, we can refine the parameters for the AI to ignore. Send that drone higher and we'll circle around these guys. Let's keep hunting."

A couple hours later as we baked in the midday heat, which was moderated but not completely eliminated by our battlesuits, Jock called in and told me they'd come across a patrol too but hadn't see anything that looked like Unity mercs. They sent the images to Ward and he concurred.

The rest of the day we sat in the shade and let Platterpussy free to wander the sky. The sun went below the horizon and we set up camp. Around midnight local time I drifted off to an uncomfortable sleep as Zelag watched the monitor for signs of wandering enemy. We weren't game for trying to scan their fortified positions but we figured at some point they'd be sending out some guys or bringing in a load of supplies or something where we might catch a glimpse of an isolated group with at least one Unity guy in it. I was having a fitful dream about electric worms eating into my brain when something shaking my shoulder woke me. I grabbed the arm, and realized from its complete lack of give that it belonged to Zelag.

"What's up, Zee?"

"We've got movement again," he said. Ward was already up and looking at the monitor.

"Bang," he shouted with satisfaction.

"Do we have one?"

"We have one," he confirmed. "Or else that truck is carrying a pair of nuclear reactors."

He pointed to the screen. Even unresolved, there was one white-hot glow in the cab and a second one toward the rear of the transport that was impossible to miss. Zooming in on the latter, we could see that it belonged to one of eight human figures in the back of the truck, but whereas the other seven resembled the standard profile we'd identified as an Axiosi regular, the eighth one looked like a being of pure light.

"I guess they come in pairs." The decision was an easy one. "Let's go get them."

We tore down the hillside at our suits' top speed, aiming to lay an ambush about a klick before the vehicle's current location. It was going to be close, since the drone image showed us they'd picked up speed.

"Get ahead of them," I yelled, as I ran like a madman, shooting a burst of stim into my system to knock back the burning of my limbs. You can run like the wind in a suit but it hurts when you do it for too long. The truck was nearing the ambush spot—and then they sped up even faster.

"They've seen us," Jones said, his breath coming in gasps over the com. "They must have sensors."

"We're just inside Feemper range," Zelag said. "Just a little farther."

We hauled it but the truck was starting to pull ahead now—we weren't going to make the cutoff point.

"Ward!" I yelled. "Crash the drone into the vehicle!"

"What about the sensor?"

"Just do it!"

Ward crouched down and pulled out his remote and we sped past him towards the truck. I could see it on my scanners and the glowing dot of the vehicle was still pulling away. They passed our intended ambush point and I heard Jones curse.

Then there was an explosion and the truck veered sideways and slowed.

"I think I winged them," Ward said on the com.

"Blast them!" I yelled. "Whoever gets closest first, open up."

Jones was ahead of me by about 50 meters with Zelag about 20 behind him. I saw the truck start to move back towards its previous track but my leg just wasn't getting me there fast enough.

"Must not have hit them hard enough," Jones shouted.

"First time... I crashed... one on purpose," Ward retorted. I could see his dot on my tactical display coming up from behind.

"I can get a shot if I get up this ridge," Zelag said. I saw him moving off to one side.

"I'm heading straight," Jones said.

Meanwhile, the truck came to a stop, then moved forward a little, then back, then forward.

"Holy Possenti," Zelag said. "I think they're stuck!"

"Firing!" Zelag yelled, lighting up the truck. Jones joined in from another angle and I kept running to get close enough for a narrow-array pulse. On my tactical display I saw a cluster of enemy signatures and a now-still truck. One of the signatures was still but the others were scattering.

"I'm gonna bet we nailed the Unity guy," I said. "Plasma on the rest!"

An explosion of lights lit up the night as I finally reached a good firing point and raised my own Feemper to my shoulder. I looked through the scope and saw multiple guys down, but nothing of the still-moving dots on my tactical display. They'd made it behind the rocks beyond the broken road and were still running.

"Alright," I said. "Move in slowly. Kill anything that moves, just try not to toast our cyborg on the ground."

We got to the truck and found the front grille smashed away on one side and the front tire torn to shreds. It was jammed up in the gravel left by some long-ago rockslide. In the back was a downed man, and another was in the cab.

"Keep your eyes open in case we have any cloaked enemy here," I said. "Ward, check out the guy in the back. I'll take the cab." I opened the driver's side door of the truck and realized the dead man was slumped in the passenger seat against the door. I lit the light on my helmet and looked at him. He was in black armor like the rest of the Axiosi. No sign of damage. The guy hadn't been killed by plasma. I went around to his side of the vehicle and popped the door. He fell onto the ground like a sack of wheat.

"Whoa," Ward said from the back of the transport. "We got ourselves one creepy-looking bastard here."

"There in a minute," I said as I unstrapped the helmet of the man on the ground. I pulled it off and saw a Unity merc staring back at me. A jolt of adrenaline jumped through me and I dropped his head, thinking he was still alive. Then I realized he had no eyelids—just two silvery spheres in a face marred by plastic and ports. There was no movement. Still, I wasn't going to get any closer for now. Maybe they could infect a guy with nanotech even after they were dead. I wasn't going to take that risk. I probably shouldn't have even touched him, I thought. Maybe even now there were nanites burrowing into my suit.

"Yeah, this guy is definitely not human," Ward said. "But he's dead, as far as I can tell."

"Leave him there. We'll let them get bagged and pulled out," I said. "Jones, Zelag—don't go too far. I don't think the enemy is coming back yet." The dots of the Axiosi were already over a klick away and still moving towards the nearest base. "Though they may bring a truck and come back for these guys if we stick around too long," I said, then dialed in to base. "Squid, Blue Team is ready for exfil. Mission accomplished."

After receiving acknowledgement from Squid, I called in to the other team and let them know the hunt was over. They sounded pissed they'd come up empty, but I'm pretty sure none of them wanted to spend another day in the heat.

"What a corrupt image of the gods," Lord General Landros said as he stood looking down at the naked bodies of the two cyborgs we'd taken from the truck. "Their very existence is blasphemy."

The skin on the corpses was pale and mottled with subcutaneous electronics and strange, bulging nodules. The skin you could see, anyways. Entire sections of their bodies were constructed out of composite material and silvery alloy and rubbery plastic.

"They believe they are gods," Captain Yost said dismissively. "The next stage in human evolution."

"Then it is time to make the environment more hostile for them here on Pyrrha," the Lord General declared. He stalked angrily from the room, slamming the door shut behind him.

Chapter 11

"You smashed my drone?" Edgerton said, looking pained.

"Had to be done," Ward said. "I'm afraid the sensor got smashed too."

Edgerton sighed and shook his head.

"Hey, it worked!" Pitt said, punching the sergeant on the shoulder. "We need twelve more, as soon as you can put them together. We've already allotted the budget. Ward, Falkland, you guys come up with any tweaks you want him to make?"

"Yeah," Ward said. "We need these scanners to work from farther away. It's one thing to buzz patrols, but sending them low over enemy encampments will just get us dead drones. No way they don't have some anti-drone laser batteries linked to an AI out there."

"Tricky," Edgerton said. "It's a close-up sort of a sniffer, you know?"

"You can't figure out a way to direct it closer?" I said. "Zoom in, somehow?"

Edgerton hummed tunelessly to himself for a few moments, looking up towards the roof of the hangar workshop. "Well," he said. "I might be able to tighten up the field. Direct it, maybe. Would have to be pretty tight to be out of range though."

"Okay," Pitt said. "Good man. Tighten it up, then."

"It will take a lot more search time on a tight beam, though," Edgerton said. "No—wait. I could just set it up to search with regular thermals, then scan the identified points. Yes, yes. Let the base AI sort and flash, kind of, just hitting the points with the sharknose once they're already seen."

"Good work, good work," Pitt said. "Hey, you want a job working for my tech team?"

"Depends on the range privileges," Edgerton grinned. "And I doubt you get the fun guns lurking around the edges of civilization."

We hashed out a plan to spot the rest of the Unity mercs by sending up our drones over the front lines of the Axiosi invasion. If we could figure out where the cyborgs were, then we could hit them however we could. We had no idea how many of them there were, but judging by the multiple times the knights fought the Axiosi without getting taken down with a nanite rifle, we figured they might be spread a bit thin. The first thing was to get the drones in the air and figure out what we were dealing with.

For two days we trained with the Sfodrian militia. Much to Yost's satisfaction, the commoners were learning tactics and starting to get some cohesion. Knowing they were now Sfodria's main line of defense instead of the long-venerated knights seemed to put some spine in them. Despite their lousy training, they were dedicated. For years they'd been little more than cannon fodder to slow enemy attacks until their big brothers showed up in massive and borderline-indestructible battlesuits. Now was their turn in the spotlight and they were determined not to blow it.

On the night of the second day, the drones took flight towards the enemy position. I watched them take off, almost silent as they floated like spirits up into the dark sky. It was late and I'd spent most of the day teaching a company of militia various formations so I hit the sack, figuring the night's work was in the hands of the drones and their masters on the ground.

I woke up early the next morning, eager to see what had happened. Ward was still asleep and the weird purple dawn was just breaking between the window slats.

I caught Edgerton in the cafeteria, looking beat. "What's up, Edgerton?" I asked.

He blinked and looked blearily over at me. "Stayed up with the drones last night, watching the info come in."

"All night?" I asked.

"Yes, just couldn't stop watching. We found some."

"Unity?" I asked. "How many?"

"Morning, Falkland," Pitt said, walking into the room with a carafe. Suddenly I smelled something good.

"Coffee again. Good man."

"Some for you too, Edgerton?" Pitt asked, pushing a mug over to me.

"No thanks," Edgerton said, shaking his head.

"Captain told me I should quit," I said to Pitt.

Pitt laughed. "Brass is brass. They don't appreciate the finer things. So, Edgerton tell you about last night?"

"Right," Edgerton said with a yawn. "They look incredible on the scanners. All glittery. We found thirteen total, and we scanned all over the place."

"That's it?" I said. "Just thirteen?"

"Yep," he said, yawning again. "That was all. Pitt can fill you in on the rest. I'm going to sleep until someone makes me wake up."

"Rest in peace," I said as he walked out. "So, Pitt—13?"

"Right," Pitt said. "And they swept again and again. We got thermals inside of buildings, then the platterpussy nailed them down. The pinpoint worked like a charm, though it did take a few passes on some. Six of the bastards are in just one building we've ID'd as a company HQ. Seven others are scattered here and there."

"They spot the drones?" I asked.

"Oh sure," Pitt said. "But they've seen the drones before. None of 'em knew these were any different. They shot one down but we got the rest back."

"Hope they didn't recover it and see our new scanner."

"Nope," Pitt said. "We blew it up ourselves."

"You can blow them up?" I said. "We could have used that feature the other day."

"That one you couldn't blow up," Pitt said. "Edgerton packed the new ones with an explosive device, just in case. They get hit or go down, they blow up. Better not to give the bad guys any idea of our capabilities, right?"

"Right," I said, finishing my coffee. "Speaking of that, where's the captain this morning?"

"He's meeting with the Lord General. Should be back in a few."

"Hey," Jones said, walking in and pouring himself some coffee without asking. "What's up with the drone scans, Tommy?"

"Edgerton says thirteen Unity mercs identified. Six are in one spot, the rest are spread out."

"I feel a special mission coming on," Jones said.

"Yeah, most like. When the captain gets back, we'll see."

Jones was right. It was a very special mission. Now we were concealed on a ridge, without our battlesuits as three of the giant knight-mechs launched an assault on an enemy position. We'd been given armor, but it was nothing like our servo-assisted suits with their AI-assisted tactical systems.

"I'll bet these cyborg bastards are licking their plastic lips at taking out three knights," Jock said from my right.

Park was watching the entry to the enemy base through the scope of his L-24 while Edgerton was glued to the readout on a sophisticated jamming field generator. The thing weighed about 20 kilos and had a self-contained AI that automatically wave-cancelled incoming scans. Edgerton was grumbling to himself as he worked its touchscreen. Before we'd left, he'd had his augment firewalled somewhere inside his brain. His brainjack had been removed, just like the rest of ours. We were even using ancient headset coms. We'd been stripped of everything the techs thought the Unity might be liable to hack and now we were going in to take them on their own turf.

For all their size and power, the knights were just the bait.

I watched the surrounding of the compound as the knights rolled into position, then unwound and took standing attack positions in front of the gate. They launched blasts of plasma that splattered off the shield protecting the multiple quonset huts inside, prompting the enemy inside to deploy and starting firing back at them. The knights' cloaking had permitted them to approach to within 100 meters before they opened fire, so to the Axiosi it must have looked like they appeared from nowhere. I watched through my scope as the shield broke down and allowed blasts of fire from the lead knight through and into the side of one of the huts, tearing through its walls and igniting the metal in a burst of radiating heat.

"We got artillery getting prepped," Ace said over the com. "Drone has eyes on a gun crew. Sir Mephiston—lock and load." Mephiston was the silver-haired knight. He'd volunteered for this mission, somewhat to my surprise. Today he would play mobile artillery.

"Acknowledged," I heard the knight say. This time, the knights had deigned to share a channel. Decent of them, really. "Coordinates?"

Ace read off a string of numbers and Sir Mephiston, his suit shining with filigrees of red on silver, took a knee and extended a gun from the back of his suit, then began to fire mortar rounds in a high arc over the buildings.

"Drop ten," Ace said, and the knight fired another extended salvo. Shells started to fall around the knights as an enemy mortar crew opened up from behind the base. One round almost nailed the knight to the far right, knocking him down for a moment as a spray of rocks slammed into him from an impact. He recovered and opened fire on the buildings again.

The shields collapsed completely as the knights continued their relentless assault, finally allowing us to get in on the action. I opened up with my Feemper on its plasma sniper setting, taking down any Axiosi I could catch in my sights. I really wished for my tactical display so I could see how many kills each of our team was making. Judging by his rate of fire, Park was probably at twice my hits already.

"Watch for Unity," Jock said. "Look for anyone with a projectile weapon, and keep an eye out for the cloakers. They've got to be coming out any second now."

"HIT!" Ace said. "The gun down. Got another one being readied, 40 meters to the right of the previous position. Don't bother with a spotting round, fire for effect!" The mortar-launching knight adjusted quickly and sent another set of shells into the new gun's position, taking it out along with its crew before they'd even fired a single shot.

"There!" Jones said. "Left side of the third quonset hut!" I jerked my scope over and spotted three mercs with nanite rifles moving forwards towards the cover of reinforced concrete barriers where they could get a shot at the attacking knights.

"Switch to EMP!" Squid ordered and we did. "K-team, pull back now!"

The two knights in my field of view fired their jets and rocketed their massive forms back 500 meters before the enemy could come within range. Then a mortar round exploded about 20 meters in front of us, scattering dust and blocking our view. "Fox Team, you've been spotted!" Ace said. "Another mortar is now operational. Sir Mephiston, please send four rounds 50 meters east-northeast of your previous target."

"Acknowledged," the knight replied. FOOMP-FOOMP-FOOMP-FOOMP!

The dust started to clear and I saw one of the Unity guys pop up with his rifle, aiming for Sir Erichsson, who had not yet fallen back with the other two knights. I sighted up, but before I could squeeze off a shot the guy went down.

"Got him," Park said coolly.

"Good shot," Jock said. "Two more back there, though. I don't know if the EMP can penetrate that barricade, even on tight-beam."

Even as he said it, I saw another merc pop up and this time I had him. ZAP! The guy froze up and fell backward like he'd been frozen in ice. He just locked up and dropped.

"Nice shot, whoever that was," Jones said.

"Target destroyed. Sir Mephiston. The mortar is knocked out," Ace said over the com. "Nice shooting!"

"Two down, four to go," Jock said.

"Jamming field is acting up," Edgerton warned. "I think we're going visible to sensors. I'm seeing some serious wave distortion."

"Stay down," Jock said. "Keep eyes on that barricade. One more guy back there. They must be EMP-hardened barriers."

"All right, Bastards, here's the skinny," Ace announced. "There are fewer guys here than I thought. Looks like we're only dealing with the HQ platoon."

"Fantastic. Let's smoke 'em," Jock said.

"Let's get in there," Squid ordered. "K-team, launch your rockets, then retreat two klicks. Wardogs, pop smoke and enter hard! We'll pick off the cyborgs."

Our teams were located to the sides of the installation. We weren't sure if they could see us, but the focus of fire was on the knights as they fell back. Their final barrage of rockets caused the enemy to put their heads down for a short while, but they were back at their posts when they saw the knights retreating. We came in from the sides fast, firing through the smoke, blasting with combined EMP and plasma at the advancing enemy.

"Another cyborg down!" Morrel said over the com.

"I've got three more of them retreating," Ace said. "They know we're after them! Towards the center of the installation now, second building from the left perimeter."

We headed in, taking down the regulars who happened to get in our way as we advanced. They weren't in the mood to put up much of a fight, as they seemed to realize the gig was up. Ward, Zelag and I got to the building first and Ward blew the door. Multiple bolts of plasma flew out at us, so I chucked in a frag. The concussion rocked the small building and the firing stopped. Zelag looked in the window. "I see two down!" he said. "Head in."

We did and saw two of the cyborgs on the ground. Their armor was scarred by the grenade explosion but their helmets were both smoking. The third was hunched in the corner, unarmed.

"Freeze, freakshow!" Ward yelled, covering him with his Feemper. The cyborg put up his hands slowly. I stripped the helmet off one of the two on the ground. Two metallic spheres fell from the helmet as I pulled it off and looked at the cyborg's ruined face. Curls of smoke drifted from ears and empty eye sockets.

"Possenti's holy mother," Zelag said. "His eyes blew out."

"They deleted their existence," said our prisoner. "As shall we."

"That's not necessary," Ward said. "We won't kill you if you cooperate."

The prisoner stood upright and shook its inhuman head. "If you attempt to forcibly extract information that is not classified as public, this unit must be deleted," the cyborg said.

"That's fine," Ward assured it. "We don't need anything from you. We won't harm you and we won't interrogate you. Look, if we don't keep our word, you can blow your own head off any time, right?"

"Your logic is correct. Deletion can be delayed, pending future events."

I looked down at the dead cyborgs on the ground, not sure why Ward thought the surviving creature would be worth keeping around if we couldn't ask it anything important. "Sounds like we have a deal," I said. "Just behave yourself and don't try to hack any of our systems. We'll treat you as a prisoner of war and you'll be released unharmed."

"Mighty sensible of you guys," Zelag said. "I'll make diplomats of you yet.

Chapter 12

We were feeling pretty good after knocking out the base and taking a live prisoner, but our elation didn't last long. When we got back to base, we found ourselves overwhelmed by a beehive of unexpected activity. Our captured cyborg was promptly delivered into the hands of four non-jacked Sfodrian MPs who escorted him away.

"Well done, men," Captain Yost said as we drove in and pulled off our helmets, looking forward to some respite. "But don't get comfortable."

"Shoot," Squid said, swigging a bottle of water. "What's going on?"

"A major enemy offensive looks to be in progress," Captain Yost said. "The Axiosi are positioning their troops to attack the capital. It very much looks like a serious assault on Nepolon is in the works. Knights and militia are mobilizing to defend the perimeter and more are coming down from Laconia. They lasered our first flight of drones from the sky but not before we observed multiple armored columns advancing from the north. I would assume the remaining Unity operatives are with the attacking forces. The Lord General was here when we got the news, so be ready for a briefing in twenty. He wants to talk to us before he returns to the Hall of Meeting to address the public. Suit up and meet me over there."

When we got back to our room I splashed some water on my face and looked at Ward, who shrugged at me. "Another day, another dollar. At least we get paid for this."

Fifteen minutes later we were in the cafeteria. Lord General Landros and multiple Sfodrian officials were there along with five knights, including Sir Mephiston. A map was projected on the rough metal wall.

"We must defend the city at all costs," the Lord General said with no introduction. "Forty knights are now preparing themselves for the defense as I speak and more will come from their estates across the polity."

"What of hacking risk?" Captain Yost asked.

"Captain," the Lord General said, "your service to the polity has not gone unrecognized, but you must realize by know that we hold our honor far more dear than any of our lives."

"How much more noble blood can you spare?" the captain replied. I thought it was a reasonable question.

"As much as it takes," one of the knights said. "Down to the last drop. No enemy may defile the sacred city."

I cleared my throat. Yost heard me and addressed the Lord General.

"Lord General, may my man be permitted to share his thoughts on the matter?"

The Lord General looked my way and I saw recognition in his eyes. He nodded.

"The knights will be the first targets, not the militia. Not the buildings. Not your infrastructure. They know of your honor and they are taking advantage of it, to your detriment. They are turning your very strength against you."

"What other option is there?" the Lord General said. "Our order stands as a shield before the people. We have over three hundred thousand commoners in the city. If we do not defend them, they will be massacred. We cannot stand by and permit that to happen. Better we die first."

"The knights are certainly the primary targets," Captain Yost observed. "Many will certainly be lost if they charge into battle. Yet still, the mercenaries are few in number and the Axiosi must know we're on to them. This reeks of panic to me."

"Lord General, I believe they're trying to force you to sacrifice your knights," I said. "Our combined approach proved highly effective earlier today. We killed all the mercenaries and not a single knight was lost."

"I confirm the hireling's words," Sir Mephiston confirmed, nodding at me in a manner that was almost friendly. "There was no dishonor in their tactics and the enemy was entirely defeated."

"Very well," the Lord General said. "The enemy approaches but is not yet at the gates. We need not commit our forces yet. Captain, if you can provide us another option, we will consider it. Nepolon must be defended, but we shall not yet decide precisely how."

After the Sfodrians had left for the Hall of Meeting, we reviewed the data coming in and discussed the options.

"Perhaps we could put the militia in front of the knights and let the knights act as artillery," Squid suggested. "That worked this morning."

"Put them behind the commoners?" Zelag said. "That won't sit well with the knights. Also, the militia isn't trained to direct them. It would be a disaster."

"Yes," Zelag said, "but certainly they realize that's suicide."

"I don't think suicide is a big deal for them," Yost said.

"They need to be there for their people," Ward said.

"Maybe…" Pitt said, trailing off.

"What?" Yost said. "Spit it."

"The Ascendancy fears nothing more than an incursion of the cyborgs," Pitt said, chewing on his lip. "They're paranoid about it. You know, if we made a call, they might be very interested in what's going on here."

"Yeah, but this is a League system," Jock said. "It's an independent planet."

"Sure," Pitt said, "but it's what, two, maybe three jumps away from an Ascendancy naval base. A few Unity mercs now, then some more advisors, then before long, there is an Axiosi nation-state dominating the world and putting the entire planet under Unity control. It's a quick slide into a full-on Unity beachhead. These mercs and their interference are likely just a test. A worm in the system, so to speak. From what I've read about the hiveminders, they're pretty subtle that way. They find a weakness and slip in, before you even know what they're up to, they already present a serious threat. And there isn't much the League is going to do about it. They're more of an economic alliance than anything else. This is out of their league, so to speak."

"Maybe," the captain said. "WDI isn't exactly in good odor with the TA, though."

"We're a legitimate corporation, publicly traded!" Pitt said, sounding offended.

"I mean the Navy," Yost explained. "And the Sfodrians are touchy and independent as hell," Yost said. "They might see the TA showing up as a threat that's worse than the Unity."

"I doubt that," I said. "It's obvious they're in over their heads. If a few mercs can show up and upset a balance that has lasted for centuries, taking out more of their leaders than have ever been lost in their history, then what would a thousand Unity operatives be able to do? This isn't a time to stand alone, as much as I hate to say it. Even if we threw the whole WDI corporation at the Unity, we couldn't win. The TA knows it's a huge threat, the Sfodrians know it's a huge threat, and we know it's a huge threat."

"We need a way to just let them know without it being on anyone's shoulders. Maybe a personal call, or maybe we just send the data to the right people in the Navy."

"I might know the right people," Zelag said. "I've still got some good connections from my days in the diplomatic corps."

"Fine," Yost said. "Send the data. Just raise it as an urgent issue of high concern. Give them our sharknose specs, too. That will sweeten the deal. Tell them to come in with sensors tuned and let them know what they're going to see. Tell them the Axiosi have gone rogue and allied with the Unity, and the Sfodrian government is too proud to ask for help. The Ascendancy Navy is always looking for possible infiltrations."

"We should have called them days ago," Pitt said. "They would have been all over this. They've almost certainly got a ship nearby already."

"It might take days to get a message to my people," Zelag said. "Maybe we should go right to the local patrol and hope for the best."

"Do both," Yost said. "We'll let the Lord General know there's a plan in the works. Now we need to figure out how to stall the bastards before they take the capital. And keep the knights from throwing themselves into the Unity rifles."

"Here is the possible problem," Jones said. "We took out almost half the remaining Unity, right, but now the Axiosi are heading in. So far, it's only been the Unity mercs launching nanites. The pattern was always the same. A few Axiosi go down, then a cyborg appears and hits the knights and turns the tide. Now there are what, seven of them left? And they're launching an assault in a situation where they know all the knights are bound to show up? There is no way seven mercs are gonna take all those knights before they get their asses blown to hell."

"True. I can't see them being that stupid," I said. "Something else must be going on here."

"I say their beta tests are complete," Park said. "I'll bet they have Axiosi snipers carrying their nanotech."

"Bingo," Jock said. "That's gotta be it. No way they're launching an offensive like this with only seven guys capable of taking down the knights. We need to assume the worst."

"Yeah," Zelag said, "What better way to draw out the knights than make a major move on Nepolon? They can't sit idly by and let the capital fall."

"They'll have to fight," Jock said. "And that's just what the enemy wants. All these skirmishes have been nothing more than a big setup."

"Well," Captain Yost said. "Let's just hope the TA decides to step in. We should make it through this if the cavalry doesn't arrive. But the knights won't, and I'm kind of starting to like those big metal bastards."

"Speaking of metal bastards, sir," I said. "Ward gave that Unity prisoner our word that we wouldn't interrogate him so he wouldn't suicide. Maybe the Sfodrians can trade him for some of their captured officers or something."

"Noted," Yost said. "I'll make sure they don't kill him."

Roughly an hour later we joined up with the militia outside Nepolon. They were streaming into camp as we arrived. Many of the men lived in the city and had just been called up and sent to armories for rifles and ammo. Those who had been training with us were more organized and we placed them over the others. Unlike many cities which flow from urban to suburban to rural without a clean line of demarcation, the Sfodrian capital was organized inside a series of squares with a huge cross highway running straight into the center of the town where a massive hundred meter wall rose up like a cliff and surrounded the 100 square kilometer plateau upon which the temples, squares, knight's villas, the Hall of Meeting and administrative buildings were located. Huge stairs went straight up from the each of the highways of the city proper to the top of the plateau. There was a vehicle access to the south, starting alongside the stair and wrapping around in a long upward inclined plane to the top, interrupted by multiple checkpoints. The heat of the midday sun baked the stone and concrete of the city and the air rippled with heat, occasionally cooled by ancient carobs, dates, figs, pomegranates, olives and other trees I didn't recognize, planted in neat squares cut alongside the stone roads and in the meagre squares of baked clay in front of houses. Beyond the edges of the city were the knights' grand estates, scattered patches of green amidst the yellow-brown dirt and scrub of the wilderness.

"We made contact with a Navy destroyer," Pitt said as we watched Sfodrian militia members scrambling to connect with their units in the field around the large base at the northern edge of the city. "They're 65 kilosecs out. They say they'll come to investigate."

"Good," Yost said. "Maybe they'll be helpful, maybe not. Current intel says we can expect the enemy assault to begin today, before nightfall."

"Got any brilliant plans?" Squid asked the captain in between contemplative puffs on his cigar.

"Maybe," the captain said. "Though it's going to rely on the militia here, and I don't have much confidence in them. Morrel thinks they'll hold, though, and we don't have a lot of options."

Morrel nodded. "No, we don't. But they do have guts and they're better than they were before we showed up."

"So what's the plan?" Squid said.

"We need to keep the knights away from the front lines," Yost said, absent-mindedly waving away a cloud of aromatic smoke. "They'll stay behind the militia positions and act as artillery, firing over their heads, launching rockets, hitting the enemy from range with everything they can throw. We'll fight until the enemy presses in heavily, then stage a fighting withdrawal through the city. The civilians are being evacuated back towards the plateau. It's possible we can hurt the enemy hard enough that they'll withdraw, or at least buy enough time until the Navy destroyer arrives. If we're lucky, they'll nuke the bastards from orbit."

"Plans that depend upon luck usually don't work out so well," I said. "What about us?"

"There are twenty-four of you and six battalions of militia. That's four per battalion, so divide up as you see fit, but keep one with the battalion CO to advise him and one with whoever is commanding the reserve. The knights will place themselves behind as they see fit. If any of them charge forward and decide to be heroes, let them go and don't try to defend them. You guys stay with your battalion and try to hold them together. We can't babysit the knights. Keep your men from breaking as best as you can, and shore up the weak spots; they'll be encouraged by your armor. Hold out as long as you can; the longer you hold, the more civilians will be out of harm's way."

Jones laughed. "If there are any women's swim teams that need some help evacuating, I'd be–"

"Shut up, Jonesy," Squid said. "What do we do if our battalion runs? Do we stick with them then?"

"Let them go," the captain said. "At that point, our job is done and you should make your way to the rally point. Once the battle is over, one way or another, we'll exfil the planet together. You've already got the coordinates to the transport."

"Got it, captain. Any idea yet how many Axiosi we're facing?"

"Twenty thousand troops is the current estimate," Yost said. "Complete with armor, artillery, and presumably those damned knight-killers."

An arcing rain of shells and plasma announced the enemy assault. Above the field spatters of energy and explosions crackled and thudded against the defensive energy shields. It was 1600 local time. To my irritation, I saw the locals starting to show signs of trying to retreat from the enemy bombardment.

"Captain Gardoros," I yelled. "Hold your men steady, let the shields do the work. Keep your men in front of the knights!" Gardoros was now designated a captain, having been promoted at some point during the last week as per the reorganization WDI had instigated.

"Yes, Lord Corporal," he replied. "We'll hold."

I could see him yelling and gesticulating as he exhorted his men on another channel. Lord Corporal? I laughed. Works for me.

To my left I watched as the militia stacked sandbags around a machine gun nest they were frantically building before the arrival of the enemy.

Another voice on my com. "Hireling Falkland, this is Sir Mephiston. We are ready for your command." It was the knight with the silver hair. I was pretty sure he wasn't going to call me Lord Corporal.

"Copy that, Sir Mephiston. I will give the signal."

The shield-generator was holding despite the enemy fire pouring in. We were a half-kilometer outside the city and it was easier to generate a field here due to the lack of structures. I did my best to remain calm even as the splashes of fire disintegrated just meters over our heads. Then the shelling slowed.

"Enemy moving forward," Squid announced over the com. "Let them have it!"

I looked at the Sfodrian tech running the shield generator. He caught my eye and held up three fingers.

"Shields down in three, two, one!" I said to the knights. "Fire!"

The shimmer of light over our heads vanished and then rockets and arcs of plasma streaked over our heads from behind as the knights opened up on the Axiosi. The front lines of the militia opened fire as well, suppressing the enemy's advance. It was Captain Yost's idea to use the knights as mobile artillery, and it was a good one. They could launch awesome arcing fire over our heads and the militia could fire away at ground level, keeping the knights in the back protected from most of the enemy fire.

"Tommy," Jones said over the com. He was somewhere in the battalion but I couldn't see him at the moment as we were spread behind walls and rocks. "Park says he's spotted multiple Axiosi armed with nanite rifles. The hunch was correct."

"Roger," I replied. "Sir Mephiston, please let the other knights know that the enemy is armed with nanite rifles. Repeat: confirm enemy regulars carrying Unity-style anti-knight weapons. Do not engage with them and stay at least 100 meters clear. One shot and you're down."

"Understood," came the response.

I hunched behind a rock next to the guy running the shield generator. The emitter was on an antigrav sled. A big box with coils on top. A fat cable ran out the back to a fusion generator on a second sled where two more techs nervously watched a status screen.

"The enemy advance has stopped and they are holding position," Squid announced. "Watch for artillery fire."

Even as he said it, a shell exploded to my right in a burst of hot pink plasma, tearing three crouching Sfodrian militia men into shreds. I could feel the heat through my suit.

"Generator up!" I yelled as more shells fell. "Shield up! Knights, cease fire!"

The techs moved to re-activate the shield, but not before another shell slammed into the ground near the fusion generator, knocking the sled sideways for a moment and taking down one of the techs. Above us there was a shimmer of light and the shield went back up. Explosions lit the air above us like boiling rainbows.

"Men, there are still civilians evacuating from behind us," Yost announced over the com. "We're going to need to buy them more time."

"Knights," I announced, "we need to hit them hard this time. When the shield is down again, target the enemy's front lines. Scouts, call in your coordinates directly to the knights' channel. Over."

The spray of fire above lessened. "Drop shields," I ordered. "Three—two—one—open fire!"

The angle of the knights' attack changed as they hit closer to the front line. The enemy advance continued, however, and was bolstered by the arrival of several armored squadrons. The tanks moved relentlessly forward towards our front line amidst the Axiosi infantry. The militia opened up with machine guns and anti-tank missiles but they were outgunned. I watched as a plasma fireball blew one crew and their gun out of a circle of sandbags to my left, sending red-hot sand flying everywhere and igniting the scrub brush for meters around the hit.

"We need to pull back!" Squid said over the com.

"We are still evacuating civilians," came a voice I didn't recognize. "We're going to need another hour or so."

"You're not going to get it. Tell them to move their asses," Yost ordered. "We are pulling back, civilians or no civilians, in one kilosec. Knights, keep the pressure on. Target the armor."

When the captain gave the signal, Gardoros gave the order to pull back, and the knights covered our withdrawal from our fortified positions. The rocky terrain, uneven ground and random farm buildings hindered their shooting, as did the disorganization of the militia. Hitting the enemy was hard under good circumstances, but from their vantage point at the back of multiple straggling and retreating columns it should have been near impossible. The whole field of battle was electronically jammed to hell, too. My tactical display was dead and I'm sure the knights must have been at least half-blind themselves, yet their firepower was still managing to slow the enemy considerably. If they hadn't been hampered by the knowledge that advancing into the midst of the enemy was certain death, this offensive would have been over by morning.

"Get the shield up and pull back into the city," I ordered, and Gardoros repeated the order to his men. The shield went back up and the knights stopped firing as we retreated into the industrial buildings that would serve as our second line of defense. I was trying to cover the guys with the shield generator and had a group of men keeping the way open for them to roll the unwieldy thing back under cover. We got it into the parking lot of a big building with huge blocks of multi-colored stone outside and the techs turned the shields on again. The coverage was sketchy in places because all the buildings and walls distorted the field, and the occasional shell got through, but it mostly held as we took our new positions.

"Enemy advancing," Squid said after a few minutes. "They're passing through the open ground we were just occupying, let's hit them!"

The techs nodded as I gave the signal. "Three... two... one... open fire!"

Arcs of plasma and flaming rockets flew over our heads again towards the enemy as the knights blasted the enemy position. I got a good spot by a rock wall along the edge of the highway, setting up between multiple slabs of marble leaning against the stone. I realized the building was some sort of monument manufacturing facility.

"Shields up again," Squid ordered and I passed on the word.

Ward joined me by the wall. "Hey, Tommy, I got a view of the right flank off the roof. It looks like they're starting to fall back. Jock is trying to hold them together but their shield generator is down.

"Hey, sir!" one of the shield techs interrupted. "Hey! Lord Wardog!"

I looked to see our own generator was smoking as another tech blasted it with some sort of fire extinguisher.

"What the hell?" I said.

"Something is messed up inside," one of the guys said. I looked closer and saw a chunk of of shrapnel had carved a ragged tear into the side of the fusion reactor.

"That doesn't look good," Ward said unnecessarily. "That thing going to blow?"

"Not if we shut it down now," the tech said. "If we keep running it, it will explode."

"How big will the explosion be?"

"It will take out most of the block."

Well, that made my decision easy.

"Kill it," I said, then opened a channel to the battalion. "Our shield is going down but we are going to hold our position. Fire at will and do not fall back until you are ordered to do so."

"These guys are going to be toast long before the Navy ship shows up," Ward said.

"Not if we can help it," I replied.

A shell exploded overhead and a cloud of thick grey smoke descended upon our position.

"They're popping smoke," Ward said. A second explosion unleashed a cloud of vision-obscuring smoke. We all understood immediately what that meant.

"The enemy is advancing," I said. No sooner had I spoken than I found myself surrounded by militia that were falling back much faster than any officer would have permitted. "Gardoros, what the hell is going on!?"

He didn't respond, so I addressed the battalion channel again. "3rd Militia, the enemy is advancing and you must hold your positions. We will retreat backwards in an orderly fashion. Your families, friends and countrymen are still evacuating. You are their last line of defense! Do not retreat until you are ordered to do so!"

I heard several acknowledgments, and the flow of men falling back was reduced, but it didn't entirely stop.

"We'll hold the enemy if we need to, hireling," Sir Mephiston reassured me. "Don't blame the commoners. They are not cut out for battle."

"Just keep firing on the enemy. I'll try to keep them from breaking up here."

"Falkland?" came Gardoros's voice over the battalion channel. "Coms were down. We are holding on here!"

"Bravo Zulu, Captain!" I told him, then switched channels. "Captain, the shield is down and we're under serious pressure here. We need to fall back soon if you want it to be orderly!"

"The area behind you is now clear for a good twelve blocks, teams," came the reply from Yost. "Stay cool and bring them back, nice and easy."

We fell back, unit by unit, with the knights continuing to hurl fire over our heads, slowing down the enemy advance. For a time, the battalion held together. Until suddenly, it didn't.

Chapter 13

A massive artillery shell exploded into a nearby building, hurling Ward and me to the ground with the force of the concussion and scattering glass and chunks of concrete across the street. The two militia men closest to us were killed instantly; only our battlesuits saved us. We were eight blocks back from our previous position and heavy fire was coming down the highway as Axiosi tanks rolled into the city. I picked myself up and straightened my helmet, then looked to see Ward doing the same.

"Hold the right flank, dammit!" I heard Captain Yost cursing Squid over the com. "Keep them together, Sergeant!"

"We're all screwed up over here, captain," came the reply, almost incomprehensible in the hail of gunfire echoing behind Squid's gravelly voice. "Lost two officers and the men are breaking. I can't hold them. Two squadrons of tanks are breaking through, over."

"Let's get over there and shore them up," I said to Gardoros. Ward nodded and we cut through an alley away from the main road, waving down members of our battalion to follow. I could see dozens of militia from the 6th Battalion running away from the advancing enemy as we ran down the alley.

"Dammit," Ward said. "They done broke!"

"We'll hold," Gardoros declared. "We're two blocks in from you. I've got two companies with me and a pair of RPG teams."

Another massive explosion blew apart multiple joined buildings a block ahead, almost blocking the alley with rubble. We moved towards it, then started climbing over. Apples and canned goods were scattered thorough the wreckage we were climbing over. I saw half the body of a man in an apron lying beneath a pile of bricks. He must have stayed behind to protect his grocery store. From artillery. Idiot.

I reached the top of a pile of rubble and started down the other side just as a tank appeared at the end of the alley, maybe two blocks ahead. We hit the ground, hoping they'd pass—but no such luck. The turret swiveled towards us.

"Get down!" I yelled. Men from our battalion were just climbing up the ruins behind us and they scattered. A plasma shell tore through the wreckage as I dove for cover.

Everything went white and I saw nothing for a moment, then I felt a hand on my neck and blinked a few times and realized I could see again. Above, a pair of tattered flags flew on a pole against the purple sky. Ward leaned over me and I realized it was his hand that had been on my neck. He was gesticulating and shouting but I heard nothing. My ears were shot and there was a sharp pain in my chest which quickly vanished as analgesic medi-foam sealed the area. I tapped my helmet and managed to switch over to speech recognition.

WARD: TOMMY DAMMIT TOMMY GET UP!

I got to my feet and staggered as Ward dragged me into a doorway. I said something to him but couldn't hear myself say it. My screen flashed.

YOST: PROTECT THOSE KNIGHTS.

THRASHER: THE MILITIA ARE ON THE RUN, CAPTAIN. OUR POSITION IS NO LONGER TENABLE.

"The knights are going in?" I said to Ward. "I can't hear a damn thing right now!"

WARD: SIT TIGHT, TOMMY. YOU'VE GOT SOME CRACKED RIBS.

I looked at my med readout and he was right. Dammit.

"I can still move," I yelled at him.

WARD: STOP SHOUTING. I CAN HEAR FINE.

I triggered a boost to the pain meds my suit was releasing and keyed the battalion channel. "Gardoros, if you're there, keep your men moving to shore up the flank! Go down three blocks, keep the retreat orderly!"

3B GARDOROS: ACKNOWLEDGED, LORD CORPORAL!

There was a vibration that shook the ground, and a massive figure suddenly flew over our heads towards the broken flank, followed immediately by two others.

"They've got no cover!" I yelled at Ward. "They're going to get fried!"

WARD: WE CAN'T DO NOTHING ABOUT THAT NOW.

I struggled upwards onto the rubble and saw a half-broken ladder leading up the side of a wall. "Let's get up top and see if we can make sense of what's going on."

I started up the ladder.

WARD: BE CAREFUL TOMMY. YOU'RE HIT.

I glanced at my med readout and satisfied myself that my internal organs were intact and nothing was bleeding too badly. "I'm fine."

We reached the roof and watched helplessly as the three knights flew over the retreating militia and opened up on the incoming enemy, taking out a tank and a platoon of men with their plasma cannons and then, one after another, the knights were hit by rifle fire, locking up and plunging to the ground like fallen archangels.

WARD: CONFIRM ENEMY REGULARS HAVE NANITE CA-PABILITIES. TELL THE DAMN KNIGHTS TO STAY BACK AND OUT OF RANGE!

"Yeah," I agreed, switching my com to the knights' channel. "Sir Mephiston, you cannot let the knights within 200 meters of the front line! Stay well behind the militia and engage at range. We just saw three of your knights go down hard. The infantry have the knight-killers. Repeat, we have confirmation that the Axiosi infantry possess knight-killing weapons! Do not engage at close-range!"

K MEPHISTON: WE WILL DO WHAT WE MUST.

I contacted Captain Yost. "Captain, the Axiosi have the nano-rifles. We just saw three knights shot down in less than 30 seconds. Please apprise the Lord General and tell him the..."

YOST: WE CAN'T HOLD THE CITY. FIVE OF SIX BATTALIONS HAVE BROKEN. LORD GENERAL IS IN THE HALL OF MEETING. HE IS NOT ANSWERING ME. FALL BACK TO RALLY POINT ALPHA.

WARD: WHAT THE HELL?

Multiple flaming projectiles flew overhead in the setting sun, deep into the city. The enemy was unleashing its big guns now. I couldn't hear the explosions, but they shook the ground beneath our feet.

"Gardoros," I said. "You've done what you can. Get your men out of there!"

I looked for a reply but nothing appeared on my screen. Dammit.

"It's you and me, Ward," I said. "Let's get to the Lord General!"

WARD: THAT'S THIRTY BLOCKS FROM HERE, TOMMY. WE MAY NOT BE ABLE TO MAKE IT.

"We'll make it," I assured him. "Let's go! Maybe we can steal a jeep or something!"

We cut through the alleys, dodging burning wreckage and the occasional potshot from the enemy advancing behind us. About five blocks in, we found a family hovercar, idling and half-loaded with suitcases. On the ground was a dead man staring blankly up at the sky next to the shelled ruin of what I assumed had been his house. A large piece of concrete had crushed his chest. He'd waited just a little too long to run.

Ward nudged him with his boot. WARD: HE WON'T MISS THE CAR.

We jumped in and tore up the highway, surprising a team of Axiosi scouts as we plowed through the middle of them. We also had to deal with people begging for rides, knots of looters, old guys with even older weapons either looking out for looters or waiting for the enemy, and a widespread state of complete chaos. Fires were everywhere and personal possessions scattered the roadsides. It was the first time I'd seen what a falling city looked like from the inside, and it was not a pleasant sight.

Eventually we made it to the edge of the citadel and saw the gates of the access road. Ward shouted at the nervous Sfodrian guards there and pointed to our suits, so they opened the gate to let us through. As we climbed to the top I looked out the window and glimpsed multiple columns of the enemy advancing through the streets, with sporadic fire coming back from the city's scattered defenders. Perhaps a dozen knights lay here and there below, destroyed by the deadly Unity nanites. Then we rounded one edge and drove under one of the great staircases where men, women and children were hauling their belongings to the top, jostling and panicking as smoke and shells flew through the air.

Finally we reached the Hall of Meeting and jumped out of the vehicle. I winced as I hit the ground, having forgotten for a moment about my busted ribs. Outside the great hall, guards held back the panicked civilians, most of whom were either screaming or crying. We pushed our way through the crowd, none too gently, until we reached the guards.

"Let us in!" I yelled through my external speakers. "We have to see the Lord General!"

The guards gaped at us, then pulled us quickly through, shoving back the crowd that tried to take advantage of the gap.

We marched in to the building and found the Lord General and seven knights standing in a circle of torches. The smell of incense filled the air. The Lord General turned and said something to me but I couldn't hear him.

WARD: HOW DARE WE WHAT? WHAT ARE YOU TALKING ABOUT, DAMMIT? WHAT ARE YOU DOING IN HERE WHILE YOUR CITY BURNS?

The Lord General said something to him and then I saw something in his hand. A black blade, glowing red with energy down the center.

WARD: YOU'RE KILLING YOURSELVES?

I suddenly realized we had just interrupted a mass suicide ritual.

"Goddammit!" I yelled. "To hell with your stupid honor!"

The Lord General pointed to a projection on the wall. It was a tactical map, and suddenly the despair of the Lord General and his knights didn't seem so insane. Waves of glowing red dots revealed that not only was the city being hit from the north, the enemy had now flanked the east and west and was streaming up the streets in three directions towards the citadel. Ward and I looked at the map in horror.

WARD: DAMN, TOMMY, HOW THE HELL ARE WE GOING TO GET OUT?

"I don't see how we are."

WARD: WELL, I'M NOT BLOWING MY HEAD OFF IN HERE LIKE THESE NUTCASES. I SAY WE FIGHT OUR WAY OUT OR DIE TRYING.

"Damn straight, Wardog!"

We had just turned our back on the suicidal Sfodrian lords and were heading back toward the exit when the lights above went dim for a moment and the ground shook.

WARD: HOLY MOTHER OF POSSENTI, WHAT WAS THAT?

"That's orbital artillery!"

We raced for the door, shoved the guards aside, and looked outside to see blasts of green fire coming down from the sky like the wrath of a furious thunder god.

"It's the TA!" I yelled. "The destroyer must have got here early!"

I ran back into the chamber and looked at the tactical map and saw the enemy advance to the back was suddenly evaporating in very large circles as the destroyer repeatedly hammered the enemy positions with its massive laser cannons.

The Lord General dropped his blade and shouted something to the knights. They rushed out of the chamber en masse.

WARD: THEY'RE GOING FOR THEIR SUITS. THEY'RE GETTING BACK IN THE GAME!

I switched over to our private channel. "Captain, you there? What's going on?"

YOST: LOOKS LIKE THE SPACE CAVALRY ARRIVED. I SEE YOU'RE AT THE HALL. LINK UP WITH JOCK, HE'S CLOSEST TO YOU.

"Let's go, Ward," I said. "Back into action!"

We left the citadel in our car and found Jock's battalion defending the retreating refugees on the stair. The enemy front lines were still pressing in but they were confused and they had lost their momentum, and every mighty green blast from above demoralized them. From the top of the citadel, rows of massive knights launched rockets down into the broken enemy as they fell back from the city. By nightfall, the city was silent.

Of course, I couldn't hear anything anyways, but I could no longer feel the ground shaking. The fire from the heavens finally came to a halt and the shooting stopped, leaving only the glow of burning buildings to light the abandoned streets of the city.

Chapter 14

The Lord General surveyed the surrendering Axiosi officers with the air of a conqueror, as if he hadn't been about to off himself in despair just a few hours before. My hearing was starting to come back but I felt like my ears were full of liquid. Words were being exchanged but it was mostly too quiet for me to hear.

"The Axiosi are going to turn over the Unity mercs," Ward told me me and I nodded. "They're negotiating a prisoner exchange now."

We were watching from the edge of a civic square, along with the rest of the Wardogs who were still standing. Morrel and Ace were both down, as was Jock, but all three of them were alive. Wardogs are hard to kill. Park had been winged and his arm hung limply at his side, but he wasn't about to miss the end of the battle, broken arm or no arm.

As we watched, a group of Axiosi turned over five Unity mercenaries to the Lord General. They had been stripped of their suits, and between their weird metal appendages and glittering eyes, their inhumanity was obvious to everyone. The Sfodrians surrounded them and guided them into a group behind the Lord General and his knights.

"Looks like they lost a few," I said.

"Yeah," Ward said. "The TA probably nailed some with that artillery."

Even as he spoke, a sleek atmo-ship circled down from above and landed neatly in the unoccupied portion of the square, decked out in blue and red colors. It was an armed transport, bristling with weapons, and it had some sort of fancy seal painted on the nose. The Sfodrians turned and stared at the new arrival as if they were unsure what to do next. I think it was the first time I'd seen the Lord General look surprised.

"Damn," Ward said. "That's not the TA!"

I was just reaching the same conclusion. A clean-cut officer in a navy blue uniform stepped out beneath the bright white emergency lights of the square. I noted the hazy red of a personal forceshield glittering around him. He was flanked by a platoon of twelve marines, armed, armored, and also sporting shields. They weren't taking any chances. And the battlesuits looked more advanced than ours.

I saw the officer look over our battlesuits and shake his head. "Who is in charge here?" he asked, his voice obviously amplified.

"I am," The Lord General responded. "Lord General Landros. I speak for the Spartocracy."

"All right then," he replied. "I see we have some Wardogs here, why don't you come on over as well. I'm sure you've got something to say for yourselves."

"Behave, gentlemen," Yost ordered over our coms. "This isn't the Navy, it's the Rhysalani. Looks like this is out of our hands now."

We set down our Feempers and walked over to where the Lord General and his knights stood with the Rhysalani officer. As I got closer, I looked at his insignia. He was an admiral.

"I am Admiral Anselm haut Glauser of His Grace's Navy, and I am here to represent the interests of His Grace the Duke of Rhysalan." He looked over at the group of silent Unity cyborgs. "It appears you have some persons of interest to us."

As he said it, the Unity mercs bowed their heads, then a moment later, jerked them back upwards in surprise and suspicion.

"Ah, your suicide cylinders or whatever they are. No, they won't work," the admiral laughed. "Not this time. We have some rather sophisticated dampening fields in place, so you will come with us, like it or not."

The Unity mercs tried to make a break for it towards the cliff wall some meters away, but they were none too gently held back by the

Sfodrian guards. The Admiral nodded to his marines and four of them surrounded the Unity prisoners, pushing them inside the interlocked forcefield of their personal shields. I noted they weren't touching them.

The admiral turned to Captain Yost and Lord General Landros. "I would request that you finish your surrender talks with the Axiosi here quickly. We will talk in two kilosecs."

He then turned around and returned to his ship, leaving us all standing there shell-shocked.

"I assume you have some sort of contract with the Sfodrians here," the Admiral said to Captain Yost, then took a sip of his cup of tea. We were standing inside the Hall of Meeting. The captain had insisted that all of us attend so there wouldn't be any scuttlebutt going around. He wasn't sure what the Rhysalani had planned, but he wasn't about to let them cut us out. "Visit strange new worlds, kill people for cash and prizes, then go home, am I correct?"

The captain inclined his head. "That's essentially correct, Admiral."

"And you," the admiral said, turning to the Lord General. "You lot found yourselves in well over your heads." He waved his hand around at the forty-odd knights in a grim circle around us. "You've ruled here for a long time. "Giant robot suits and all that, very good stuff. Not good enough, unfortunately."

The Lord General looked more grim than he had when he was in the middle of killing himself. He gave the Admiral the very faintest of nods, but even that effort clearly cost him dearly.

"Never mind all that now. We have a serious problem with those posthuman lunatics ourselves," the admiral said. "Bloody devils give the Ascendancy a dickens of a time and they have given the Duke more than their fair share of the heebie jeebies. I understand why you hired the Wardogs, they're not a bad option, but the fact is that you will need a lot more than a handful of mercenaries to face the Unity."

"We didn't know who we faced," the Lord General snapped. "And we have defeated our enemies many, many times on our own."

"But you had to know something was up," the admiral continued. "Something that you couldn't handle. Though you didn't hire very many guns, now did you?" He looked around at us with a raised eyebrow. "A platoon, then? Unless you have some stashed away somewhere."

"A platoon," Captain Yost confirmed. "We worked in an advisory position."

The Admiral smiled slightly and raised a hand. An aide refilled his tea and he took another sip. "Well then, it seems your advisory position would have ended rather badly for both parties if we hadn't decided to crash the party and put an end to the affair. Did you manage to catch all the cyberdevils, then, or will we have to round them up?"

"We have them all," the Lord General said. "Our technicians provided us with a scanner capable of detecting their heat signatures."

The captain reached over and very gently gripped Edgerton's arm before he could say anything. I wasn't sure what had outraged the tech more, the fact that the Sfodrian lord had just taken credit for his invention or the way in which he'd described it incorrectly. It could go either way, I figured.

"Very good," the admiral said. "That could prove quite useful. We'll ask you for the specs before we leave."

"This guy is something else," Jones muttered over our personal channel.

"Yeah, but we'd probably be dead if they didn't show up," Zelag said back.

"Shush," Squid cut in. "Talk later."

"And, of course, since His Grace the Duke of Rhysalan is not in the business of providing charity, we'll be generous and split the fee with Wardogs Incorporated. We'll also take the prisoners, of course, since they're of no use to you."

"Split our fee?" Jock shouted in disbelief. "We worked our asses off for weeks, training up their militia and saving the damn knights, putting our blood and sweat on the line and you want to–"

There was a rousing rumble of agreement from me and the other Wardogs. We'd done the hard work, and this Rhysalani just waltzes in and expects half the take for his trouble? Hell no!

Captain Yost didn't say anything at first. He was obviously thinking the matter through. He opened his mouth to speak but was interrupted by an unexpected party.

"We also object," the Lord General said.

The Admiral looked at him quizzically. "You do, do you?"

"Yes," the Lord General said. "We do."

"As do we all," said Sir Mephiston. "The hirelings have fought with honor, and even in their failure they would have died with honor. Now you seek to rob them of their coin?"

The Admiral shrugged. "You would all be dead without us. If not worse. And His Grace the Duke, as I said, and apparently must say again, does not do charity."

"Take the prisoners," the Lord General said. "We can recompense you for your fuel and your armaments expenditures as well. But we had no contract with you."

"Do you know, I thought you might say something to that effect," the Admiral said. "Let me remind you that your planet is now being orbited by the *Berchtold*, a Vulkan-class destroyer. I believe you had a ship of your own before, did you not. I understand it developed some navigation problems of some kind. Suffice it to say that we currently hold the uncontested high ground."

He smiled and stretched. "Let us all step outside for some fresh air, shall we?" He walked out and we all trailed after him, wondering what he had in mind. Outside the Hall of Meeting, the dry wind whistled past us and we looked down at the recovering city. The fires were mostly under control now and the power was beginning to be restored here and there.

"What are we doing out here, Admiral?" the Lord General said angrily. "We are men of honor, not merchants in uniforms. We made a deal with these mercenaries and we do not intend to permit you to break it."

As if in answer, a massive stream of green light came down from above, blasting a huge crater into the hillside just outside the city, shaking the ground and blinding us all for a moment with its intensity. It left behind a massive pit, steaming as the waters of the aquifer poured into its molten center.

"I would have moved the impact a little closer into town for maximum effect," the Admiral said to the officer next to him. "Could have made a very nice lake for a city park, I think. Have the gunner make an adjustment, please." He turned back to the Lord General. "Pray, continue, Lord General Landros. You were saying?"

The Lord General said nothing, his jaw working up and down for a moment, then finally he managed to speak. "We will give you what you ask," he said at long last. "We are deeply appreciative for your gracious intervention against the Axiosi, and we have decided that your terms are eminently reasonable."

The Admiral nodded. "Thank you. On behalf of His Grace, the Duke of Rhysalan, I accept. We'll take care of the paperwork."

He looked at Captain Yost. The captain smiled grimly. "The strong do what they can and the weak suffer what they must."

"Ah, an educated man!" said the Admiral, looking delighted. "Wonderful! You must dine with me tonight, Captain. I'm certain we will have much to discuss."

"What just happened?" Ward elbowed me.

"We just took a pay cut," I explained.

"Half a loaf is better than none," I told the others, a little too loudly judging by the way everyone looked at me. My ears were still ringing.

We were strapped in on a rattling old atmospheric transport headed back up to the spacedock. I sat in between Zelag and Pitt. My hearing was better after a little work from a doc, but it wasn't fully recovered yet. My ribs were bound up and aching, but they would heal. Sometimes, just surviving counts as a win. If a platoon of Wardogs disappeared on an independent world out in the boondocks, no one was going to care except for their significant others and the legal team back on Kantillon. You have to take what you can get.

"I'm a little disappointed things came to a head so soon," Pitt said. "I just about had the labeling system finished up at our warehouse."

"Do you think we'll get our completion bonus?" Zelag asked.

"Who knows," I said. "Maybe half, unless they say we don't merit it because the Rhysalani intervened."

"They probably won't cut it altogether," Pitt said. "At least I hope not."

"I hope we get it," Zelag said, clenching and unclenching his robotic arm. "I think I might switch this thing out for an honest-to-god human arm when we get back."

"Really?" I said. "I thought you liked beating Park at darts."

"Yeah," Zelag said. "But those Unity guys give me the creeps. I don't want to turn into one of them."

"Naw, you're fine, Cyborg," I said, thumping him on the arm. "Maybe you can be a diplomat to the machine mind."

Zelag made a face. "Hell no. Last thing I want is them hacking my arm."

"I wonder what the TA will think when they finally show up on Sfodria," Pitt mused. "They got scooped by Rhysalan. I talked with one of their marines for a bit. They'd been out for weeks on patrol when they intercepted our transmission."

"Good thing they did," Zelag said. "But I'll bet we haven't seen the last of all this."

"What do you mean?" Pitt said. "You think the Unity will come after WDI?"

"No, they don't care about us," Zelag said. "But you saw what a platoon of them could do to a moderately advanced society. Those knights were the planetary apex predators for centuries and they got put down fast and hard. What if they'd gotten into our augments? What if they hacked our HQ on Kantillon? Total chaos would ensue. It's no wonder the Rhyslani have a hard on for those freaks. For all that Admiral's arrogance, they didn't sent him to snake half our contract. They sent him because they know the gig is up for humanity if the posthumans can just get a foothold somewhere."

"The Unity have their own worlds," Pitt said with a shrug. "They haven't seriously ventured out of them in centuries."

"They just did," Zelag said. "And they just about took a whole damned planet with what, thirteen guys?"

"Good point," I said. "But it was just a small backwater planet, nothing like Rhysalan or one of the Ascendancy's worlds."

"That's how you do a test," Zelag said. "If I were them, I'd say it was a big success. If they're at all logical, which I'm sure they are, with their computer brains and hivemind and all, then they probably learned a lot from that little foray."

"So what do you think that means?" I asked him.

He stared off into the distance for a moment, saying nothing.

"Come on," Pitt said. "What does it mean?"

"War," Zelag told us. "Interstellar war."